*Pulp
and
Paper*

The

John

Simmons

Short

Fiction

Award

University of

Iowa Press

Iowa City

*Josh
Rolnick*

*Pulp
and
Paper*

ISBN-13: 978-1-60938-052-6
ISBN-10: 1-60938-052-5
LCCN: 2011925182

University of

Iowa Press

Iowa City

Josh
Rolnick

Pulp
and
Paper

University of Iowa Press, Iowa City 52242

Copyright © 2011 by Josh Rolnick

www.uiowapress.org

Printed in the United States of America

In the story "The Carousel," two short quotations come from
descriptions of longtime carousel operator Mike Saltzstein
that were contained in his *New York Times* obituary.

The University of Iowa Press is a member of Green Press
Initiative and is committed to preserving natural resources.

Printed on acid-free paper

ISBN-13: 978-1-60938-052-6
ISBN-10: 1-60938-052-5
LCCN: 2011925182

To Marcella

That's another thing this story is about,

I suppose: how there's no going back.

—ETHAN CANIN, America America

Contents

ACKNOWLEDGMENTS

Some of the stories in this collection first ap-
peared elsewhere, in slightly different form:
"Funnyboy" in *Bellingham Review*; "Inn-
keeping" in the *Florida Review*; "Pulp and
Paper" in *Harvard Review*; "Big River" in
Western Humanities Review; "Big Lake" in
Arts & Letters; "The Carousel" in *Gulf Coast*.
   I would like to thank the following people
for their help with the stories in this collection:
Greg Rienzi, Matt Williamson, Nic Brown,
Matthew Vollmer, Austin Bunn, Nina Siegal,
and Nam Le. Thanks to my writing teachers,
Mark Farrington, Robert Olen Butler, James
Hynes, James Alan McPherson, Marilynne
Robinson, Lan Samantha Chang, Ethan Canin,
and especially, Harvey Grossinger. Thanks to
Yiyun Li for selecting this book for the John
Simmons Short Fiction Award. Thanks also
to Connie Brothers, Deb West, Jan Zenisek,
David Hamilton, James McCoy, Rebecca Marsh,
Charlotte Wright, Allison Means, Karen Copp,
and everyone at the University of Iowa Press.
   For their endless inspiration, humor, and pep
talks, thanks to my sisters, Becky Rolnick and
Jenn Borchetta, and for their enduring sup-
port, to Gertrude Kleinman, Chuck Kleinman,
Marsha Kleinman, Toby Kleinman, Bob Adler,
Barbara Wolfson, the cousin mafia, Frank
Borchetta, Brian Fox, Ruth Greenspun, Joe
and Pam Kanfer, Maggie and Phillip Nabors,
Mamie Kanfer Stewart and R. Justin Stewart,
Abraham Nabors, Jonda Bechter, Ketti and
Donny Zigdon, Jaron Kanfer, Gabe Nabors,
Sylvia Lewis, Janette Kanfer, Betty and Lester
Nabors, my fabulous nephews, niece, cousins-,
aunts-, and uncles-in-law, Mae Blocker, Lal
Puri, Ben Stewart, Gerald Burstyn, and the

men of Whiskey Wednesday. Thanks to everyone at *Targum*, who taught me to stay late and
dream big dreams. To Ythamar Grose-Chaney,
for peace of mind. To my uncle, Jonathan Kleinman, for *Charlie and the Chocolate Factory*,
one chapter at a time. To my parents, Margaret
and Jerome Rolnick, who have loved, encouraged, and believed in me unswervingly since
"Daggar the Ground Monster." Finally, thanks
to Meyer Paz, Heshel Rom, and Lev Beari, for
a story every day, and to Marcella, for your
hyphens and your heart.

In memory of Milton Kleinman.

New
Jersey

Funnyboy

I glanced out the window as my train pulled into the station and saw the girl who killed my son. I recognized her ponytail — the way it shot up and bent over on itself — from the newspapers. She stood on the New York–bound platform in a hive of girls, several of whom wore West Village varsity football jackets. Missy Jones wore a pink ski vest over a white turtleneck; her blue jeans tucked neatly into white moon boots ringed with fur. She smoked melodramatically, tilting her chin up and blowing her plume at a mock Victorian lamplight. As my train came to a halt, Missy tossed her head back and laughed, flashing her teeth in the mustard light.

I turned from the window, buttoned my coat, lifted my brief-case. *She doesn't seem very contrite,* I thought, stepping off the train and starting down the platform. *She seems to be coping rather nicely, in fact.*

The train pulled out, and I queued behind people funneling into the station. When the last car cleared, a rhythmic clapping rose from across the tracks. I turned and saw the girls standing in a circle, clapping with their hands straight up, as if in prayer. A moment later they began a cheer, their voices echoing off the brick-faced station house:

> *We ain't bad*
> *and we ain't cocky*
> *gonna ride on you like a Kawasaki*
> *vroom vroom, two, three, four*
> *vroom vroom.*

I stepped out of line. The girls started again, louder. They swiveled their hips and clapped to every other syllable, then gripped the handlebars of imaginary motorcycles, twisting up the speed with each *vroom.* They stepped to the four-count—forward, left together, right together, back. When they were finished, bless their cotton-candy hearts, they whooped and hollered, their war cries reverberating under the awning, and Missy said, "Uh huh, uh huh, uh huh uh huh uh huh!"

I walked to the yellow danger line and bellowed across the tracks: "Missy Jones."

The ruckus ceased. Missy stepped out of the huddle and peered across the tracks. It took her a second, then her smile vanished. "Mr. Stern?"

"Yes, it's me," I said. "Richie's dad."

The girls shrunk together behind her, a wild herd sensing threat. "Oh, hi, Mr. Stern."

"Where are you girls off to, this fine night?"

"We're going to see *Phantom.*"

"*Phantom!* Gee, that sounds like fun."

She hesitated, then nodded. "Yeah. I've seen it before. It's one of my favorites."

"Well, see it again for the first time, *Missy.* Vroom vroom!"

I raised a fist in the air, offering a triple shake of an imaginary pompom, then whirled and headed for the station, a zesty bounce to my step. And why the hell not!

Hadn't I just single-handedly ruined Missy Jones's night?

By now I hear you saying, Spill it already. What's this all about?

So here it is. On an unseasonably warm February day ten months before I spied Missy Jones en route to Broadway, my twelve-year-old son Richie retrieved his Huffy from the garage and pedaled out into the sun-dappled streets of West Village, New Jersey. He most likely went down to the high school and cut through the parking lot, then barreled past the Quonset hut and hit the Indian trail with a full head of steam, dodging trees in the settling twilight. He shot out onto Hill. The only problem: Mrs. Edelson had died. On that unseasonably warm afternoon, her children were moving her belongings out of her home, and someone had parked a moving truck along the curb. Perhaps Richie noticed the treasure chest logo on the truck before blasting into the street between truck cab and garbage dumpster.

Missy Jones, daughter of a village alderman, was on the other side of that truck, driving in her parents' shiny Acura Integra, Candy Apple Red. She slammed on the brakes—left twenty-one feet of tire tread seared into the asphalt—and, still, she struck Richie broadside. My son flew through the air, over a plaid sofa, and hit his head against the pavement of Mrs. Edelson's driveway. Her forty-two-year-old son, I am told, heard the sound of Richie's head hitting the concrete and vomited into the azaleas.

Missy Jones was seventeen, a West Village High School junior. The entire episode was extremely unsettling to her. She was so distraught, in fact, that she quit the cheerleading squad. She had lost her mirth, you see; she couldn't locate that special place deep inside where spirit lives and breathes. She told us this. She sent Anne and me a letter two months after the accident. It was actually less a letter than a heavily perfumed run-on sentence with postage. Missy told us how sorry she was and she wasn't speeding and she never saw him coming on the other side of that moving van and our son is a beautiful boy and she has nightmares now in which she takes a rest under a tree in an open field and she looks up and there are dead children hanging from the branches. I'm not trying to be a one-man soap opera when I tell you the letter was streaked with tears.

Four months later, another letter arrived. Missy wanted to meet with us, to apologize in person, or, as she put it, "broken heart to broken hearts." Anne's instinct was to forgive, as it always is. She told me about the ancient Samoan ritual of *ifoga*. In that culture, it seems, when one person seriously wronged another, the wrong-doer, along with his or her family, would go directly to the home of the aggrieved. They would bring oven stones, wrap fine mats over their heads, and kneel, as a group, at the doorstep, prostrate for hours or even days in the hot Pacific sun, while the injured family deliberated over whether to accept the apology. Eventually, the family's Talking Chief would come out, accept the mats and stones, and invite the other family inside. It was a risk, though. In some cases, the Chief would emerge only to lop off the penitent's head with a battle-axe.

"That's what she's doing, Levi," Anne had said. "Offering herself up."

Anne wrote Missy a note back, inviting her and her parents over for tea. But I wanted no part of it. I spent the appointed afternoon at the bar of the Swing Back Lounge.

And now, I would like to tell you what happens when your son gets hit by a car while riding his bike and then dies. For a while, there is genuine sympathy. People you don't know come to your house with tuna noodle casserole. The phone rings so often you have to shut it off before you go to bed. You get crayon drawings from school children. One little Picasso sent us a picture of a stick bicycle, broken in two, with tears streaming from the handlebars. But then things change. The cops let it be known that after a complete investigation, the accident is your son's fault. Read: *his parents' fault*. Your son becomes the poster child for reckless biking. The police chief and mayor join forces in announcing a new bike safety program. Thereafter, whenever you run into your neighbors, they blame you for the whole goddamned thing. They don't say it to your face, of course. They whisper it to each other, standing in front of mist-shrouded iceberg lettuce at the ShopRite. *He's the one whose kid was riding without a helmet!*

You'll be glad to know this story has a happy ending. Fairy tales do come true! In her senior year, confronted by the insistent pleas of her classmates, an emotionally bruised Missy Jones agreed to come back to the cheerleading squad—as the cocaptain, no less!—in time for the season opener against Ridge. Perhaps you saw her picture in the paper? The one with the sassy ponytail, come-hither eyes, and lynx-like smile?

Missy phoned several times asking to speak with me. But I refused to take her calls. Once, I drove home after work only to find Missy's cheery beery bim bom Acura parked outside. *That* car in front of *our* house! I didn't stop. As I rolled by, I saw Anne through the bay window, holding her shirt at the neck. Later, she told me Missy had stopped by unannounced. I told Anne if I ever came home and found Missy sitting in my living room, I could not be held accountable for what I might do.

"What should I tell her, Levi?"

"Tell her the truth. I'm not going to see her, and that's that."

"She's just a *kid*, Levi. She's suffering."

"Jesus, Anne," I said. "I'm suffering too."

Do you know that I no longer enjoy doing the things that we used to do together, Richie and I? Like fishing. I no longer enjoy hooking a worm through the meatiest part, so that the barb punctures the skin on the other side, and then rearing the line back, releasing the bailer, waiting for the rod to shimmy. Believe me, I've tried. The smell of earth and rich roots gets up my nose and makes me sick.

Quick quiz: What is the name of the light stripe that separates an earthworm's head from its tail? Time's up. It's called the clitellum. Do you know how I know that? Of course you don't. My son taught me that. He also taught me that, when nightcrawlers are cut in half, they don't die. They regenerate.

Imagine that. Losing half of yourself and becoming whole again.

There is a thing that crawls in the dirt and eats shit that can do that.

I was preoccupied as my train pulled into the station. It was Friday night, one week after my little over-the-tracks repartee with Missy Jones. On Fridays, I picked Anne up across town at the anthropology building, and, on our way home, we stopped off for Chinese and a Blockbuster DVD. I shuffled down the platform, into the station, onto the escalator, thinking about how in days of yore, subgum wonton and a new release had been a preamble to lovemaking. That's when I saw them, visible just beneath the ceiling at the bottom of the escalator: white moon boots ringed with fur.

That couldn't be Missy Jones, I thought. The escalator dropped down, revealing the Wearer of the Boots from the bottom up: tucked-in jeans, long legs, piglet-pink parka. *What are the chances of running into her twice in one week?*

Not until I saw the tippy-top of her ponytail; not until she scrunched up her shoulders, smiled, and waved, a fluttery little Beauty Queen wave; not until she said, "Mr. Stern! Hi ya!" did it occur to me: Chance had nothing to do with it.

You might say that what I did next was instinctual. Lions and tigers and bears type shit. I turned and bolted up the down escalator, pushing my way through a phalanx of commuters. From the top, I saw Missy running—quite speedily, to be frank—up the up escalator. She held some sort of case at her side. "Mr. Stern! I just want to *talk.*"

That's when—how did Richie used to put it? Ah yes. *I ran like diarrhea.* Down the platform, down a staircase to street level; under a train bridge and across the road.

Just before ducking into the parking deck, I chanced a glimpse back over my shoulder. Missy Jones blasted out from under the bridge, spotted me, hurtled forward. I ran into the parking deck vestibule and hit the stairwell, taking two steps at a clip. At Level 4 I threw open the door and made a beeline for my car.

I suppose you think me cruel for avoiding Missy Jones. The poor dear, you say! She just wanted closure! All I have to say to you is, sometimes a thing that looks heartless from one angle makes a lot of sense when viewed another way.

Richie was our only child. Maybe you knew him? He had curly brown hair that his mother hated to cut. Maybe you saw him down at the pond hunting toads with his butterfly net? Or throwing jet black crickets into spider webs? He was the one crouching in the reeds flicking the hair out of his eyes. If you knew him, let me tell you something: You didn't know him.

When Richie was nine, Anne and I took him to Yankee Winter Weekend at Old Sturbridge Village. On our first night, he asked to go to a magic show. The Great Something-dini was performing in Puritan Hall. We got there early and sat in the front row, and as we waited, the house filled to overflowing. When the Great Something-dini glided down to the stage on a floating unicycle, Richie was transfixed. You must understand I am not exaggerating. My child did not blink.

Toward the end of the show, Something-dini took off his black top hat and stared out into the audience.

"Now," he said, flipping the hat over three times, "I need an *assistant!*"

Richie took a quick breath, astonished. Was it possible!

The magician peered into the bright lights as a titter ran through the audience. But it was a foregone conclusion. He had picked Richie out the minute he floated on stage. A curly-headed, slack-jawed, big-eyed boy in the front row? There was never any question.

"Young man," he said, "will you please step onto the stage?"

Richie dashed to the magician's side.

"What is your name?"

"Richie."

"Richie!" He bowed with an exaggerated flourish. "May I implore you, Richie, to help me perform a staggering feat of magic?"

Richie nodded, mouth open. At this point I should mention that a slight wave of nervous laughter rippled across the rows. Perhaps the audience felt for Richie, the unwitting foil. For all we knew, he was about to be sliced in half. A full hour after his bedtime!

"Will you do exactly as I say?" The magician bent down, glaring with jade eyes. His thin, white-powdered face stopped just a few inches from our son's.

"Yes, Sir."

"Richie, I want you to look into this hat." He brandished it under Richie's nose.

Our son peered into the ethereal black depths.

"Are you *looking*?" he bellowed.

Richie pulled his nose back and nodded, shifting on his feet.

"Now!" the Great Something-dini said. "I want you to tell everyone, what . . . is . . . in . . . this . . . hat!"

Richie squinted. He stood on his toes and craned his neck way out over the hat. Then he turned, looked out at the audience, and said: "What . . . is . . . in . . . this . . . hat."

For a moment: silence. The audience was not sure whether the line was a misstep or a joke. But then Richie smiled. And the audience erupted! Laughter ripped across the hall like a Skittles top, applause reverberating off massive wooden ceiling beams. The magician certifiably blushed. The trick was on him! And then he smiled, grudgingly—but, if you ask me, in true admiration. He stepped aside and motioned to Richie with an open palm, acknowledging him as one would a trusted sidekick. "Ladies and gentleman," he said, "give it up for Funnyboy!"

And Richie? He looked out at an audience whose collective heart he had won, doffed an imaginary cap, and bowed.

Was I surprised? Yes, but also no. When Richie was four, Anne asked him what he wanted to be when he grew up. Without hesitation he replied: "A joker." Such a noble calling! And yet Anne and I secretly fretted, because at first, all of his jokes had one thing in common: They were not funny.

Here is one of his early favorites:

"Knock knock."

"Who's there?"

"Richie."

"Richie Who?"

"Richie Potato Head!"

How did Anne and I react to this? We laughed, of course! And Richie laughed too. And since Richie laughed, we laughed some more. We wanted to encourage him, you see. Being a joker in today's world is no easy thing.

And then one day, Richie strode home from school as if he had just been to the mountaintop.

"I have a joke."

"Okay, Honey." Anne chopped an onion. "Go ahead."

"Why did the apple kiss the banana?"

"Why?"

"Because it had appeal."

Well, at this, we did exactly what we always did. We laughed! This was our Little Dangerfield after all! We were not going to stand with the critics just because our son happened not to be funny. Only, after a few seconds, something happened. Both of us realized at the same time: This joke was . . . *funny*. The banana had a peel! Oh glory day! Little Richie had told a *funny* joke! And, oh, did we laugh then. I roared, holding my stomach with two hands. Anne laughed so hard she cried. Or maybe it was the onion. Or maybe she cried for some other reason. Anne's tears were the size of grapes.

Wait a minute, you say. The joke's not *that* funny.

I'm sorry to tell you, you are missing my point.

─────────

I reversed out of my stall in the parking deck and headed down, wheeling around corners, tires squealing. At ground level, I drove up behind two vehicles in the EZ Park lane, rolled down the window, waited. "Come *on*."

For a few seconds, my line did not budge. I leaned on my horn. "For Christ's sake, lady, come *on*!"

That's when she ran out onto the ramp. She stood for a moment, catching her breath, the case swinging at her side, scanning the cars. She saw me and began jogging. Two or three cars had already pulled up behind me. And what the hell was I going to do anyway? Reverse through the parking deck to the roof? And what then? Leap for the moon?

Missy came up the ramp until she was even with my car door, a few paces away. "I just want to talk to you, Mr. Stern."

I stared straight ahead. The gate opened, releasing a car onto the street. I inched up, Missy walking beside me. "Just this once. Then I won't bother you ever again."

The final car slid out, and I pulled forward, leaving Missy in my taillights. I reached out, swiped my card. The gate lifted.

Missy said: "I could have stopped."

I tapped the accelerator, then slammed the brake. In my rearview, I saw Missy standing in a billowing cloud of exhaust.

I leaned out the window and turned. "What did you say?"

"I could have stopped the car," she said. "Before . . . before the accident."

Somewhere behind me, a horn bleated twice.

"You were speeding."

"Well, no, it's not so simple. Can we talk?"

A bigger car beeped, deeper. I hit unlock, spoke straight ahead. "Get in."

She ran around behind the car, opened the door, and dropped onto the seat, accosting me with some kind of Eau de Mandarin-Musk. I pulled out, drove toward an intersection, breathing through narrowed lips. "You've got five minutes to tell me what the hell you're talking about."

"I need more than that." She watched me, intent. "There's some things I need to tell you. Can we go someplace? Maybe Shaffer Hill?"

I pictured sitting with her on the bluff, my headlights staring over the edge, the sluggish river below, and my fingertips tingled. *Get someplace public*, I thought. *Fast*. Half a block away, an old railcar diner splashed the sidewalk fluorescent.

"Missy," I said, "this had better be fucking good."

I sat on a vinyl bench at Mitch's Diner. The eatery had a *Bull Durham* theme. There were framed black-and-whites of Kevin Costner, Susan Sarandon, and Tim Robbins on the wall, each one of them signed. The menu offered a "Crash Reuben" and an open-faced turkey sandwich called "The Bigs." I ordered a coffee; Missy, a cup of hot cocoa. Drinks arrived in ceramic mugs with the Durham Bulls logo on the side.

I sat on a vinyl bench at Mitch's Diner across from Missy Jones. I leaned forward, elbows resting on the table, cupping a hand over a fist. Missy sat posture perfect.

"Mr. Stern, I really appreciate this."

I brought my fist down against the tabletop, rattling a plastic ashtray, and she flinched. "Alright already, Missy. Why don't you tell me what you have to say."

Her hand went to a strand of frizzled blond hair at her temple, and she started rubbing it back and forth. "This is hard."

"I'm sure."

"So I'll just say it."

"That'd be best."

"I looked down," she said. "Before the accident. I looked down to change the radio station."

I nodded, pressed my fingers together, turning the nail rims white.

"A Sinéad O'Connor song came on Z-100—'Nothing Compares 2 U'?—and I hate that song. I mean, I like it, but it makes me sad. So I turned to PLJ, only, I went too far. Static came on loud. I looked down—just for a second—to tune it in. When I looked up, Richie was right in front of me."

She paused, swallowing hard. "I've thought about this a million times, Mr. Stern. I keep thinking, if I hadn't looked down, I could have swerved. Or stopped."

"That's it?"

"Well, yeah."

"You looked down?"

Her forehead glistened, reflecting neon red from a "Malts" sign in the window. "I didn't want to hear that song."

"Missy, how do I know you weren't drunk?"

"I wasn't! The breathalyzer . . ."

"Or stoned, Missy. How do I know you weren't high as a kite?"

"I don't smoke."

"Right. Why should I believe you? Give me one good god-damned reason. You killed my *son*, Missy."

She pressed her lips together, held my gaze, and then nodded, almost imperceptibly. Behind the counter, a milkshake machine clicked on, churned, blended through something frozen, clicked off. "My parents told me not to tell anyone any of this," she said, finally. "My dad sat me down with a lawyer. He said if I told you or Anne, you'd sue me, and I'd screw up my life even more. They don't know I'm here. They think I'm at the mall with the team."

"So why are you telling me?"

Her eyes opened wide. "I had to."

"Why?" I slapped the table. "It doesn't change a goddamned thing." Behind the counter, our waitress glanced up at me, her brow furrowed.

"But it's what happened," she said. "I thought you'd want the truth."

The truth! And what was I supposed to glean from this truth? Sinéad O'Connor killed my son? Manual radio tuning killed my son? A Z-100 DJ behind a soundproof window at the top of the Empire State Building killed my son? What good is truth if it illuminates nothing?

I looked across the tabletop at Missy Jones. She looked nothing like the girl in the newspaper photo. She wore no makeup. Her eyes were too big for her head, and her mouth too tight. Her teeth had a yellow cast, and they were misaligned—one forward, the next one back, and so on—giving an impression of decay. She was not a natural blonde; her roots were brown. Fine strands of hair sprung loose at her forehead and neck, beneath the ponytail, which was held in place, I now saw, by a series of colored bands. The ponytail was not so much haughty as it was ridiculous. When she wrapped her fingers around her mug, her nails were unpolished, gnawed; her fingertips, red, raw.

The waitress returned to the table with a coffeepot. She looked at Missy. "Everything okay here, Hon?"

Missy nodded. "Yeah, we're okay. Thanks, Ma'am."

She refilled my cup, spilling coffee into the saucer. "You sure?"

"Yeah."

"You let me know if you need anything."

Missy fingered her mug, turning it side to side. "The thing I really wanted to tell you is that I knew him. I met him at the Paw Creek game last year." She eyed her cocoa, as if the memory was in there somewhere. "Biggest game of the year. Bleachers packed. In the third quarter, we set up for the Pyramid. Normally, the senior captain is on top. But Shelly had sprained an ankle, and the team voted, and I was the one who got to fill in.

"I was so excited, waiting for it all game." She let out a short laugh. "Only, when Shelly finally called for it, I couldn't do it.

Jimmy and Lorenzo kept trying to throw me up with the cup move, but I couldn't get my balance. I kept falling back. I had done it *so* many times in practice. I don't know. I was nervous, I guess."

She leaned forward. "After a few tries, I could hear people laughing in the bleachers. I got tight. They kept hoisting me, but I couldn't stick it. The girls were having trouble holding it together. The whole pyramid was *wobbling*. They gave me one last lift, and I thought I was going to nail it. But the Pyramid just crumbled away. There were girls all over the track. We jumped up and put our pompoms in the air, like Coach K taught us. Went straight into the Boss cheer. Like that's how we *planned* it."

I threw myself against the bench. "Missy, what's the point of all this?"

"I'm getting to the part about Richie."

"Yeah, well, get there."

Her tongue made a cameo between her lips. "The thing is, Mr. Stern, everyone knew I screwed up. I let everyone down—Coach K, the girls, the whole *school*. We won the game—Bryce ran back a punt on the last play—but afterwards, all I could think about was that Pyramid."

Now I remembered: Richie bursting into the house after the game, acting out the final punt return, imitating Bryce's shake-and-bake; leaping over a chair, a Paw Creek defender, spiking an imaginary ball into the kitchen floor, striking the Heisman pose.

"I didn't want to be around *anyone*. The girls were going to Gino's, but I couldn't deal. I said I had a headache. Then I left, out back, behind the locker room.

"That's when I saw Richie walking along the path by the Quonset hut. I had seen him around at the games. He and his friends were always hunting arrows under the bleachers—the ones we lost in archery practice? But I wasn't in the mood to talk. I just put my head down and kept going.

"He passed me, and I got this feeling like he had stopped. Like he was watching me. I thought he was going to make a crack about the Pyramid. Some of those kids can be real *brats*—whistling, snotty comments, boob jokes. That kind of thing.

"But Richie says, 'Hey, kid . . .' and then he pauses, and I don't know why, but I turned around, and he says: 'Catch!'—like from that Coke commercial? The one where that little boy gives Mean Joe Green his Coke, and Mean Joe throws the boy his shirt?"

I nodded. *Sure I know. Richie loved that commercial.*

"Only, he didn't throw me a shirt. He threw me an arrow."

A snort escaped my nose. "Richie."

"I caught it. I smiled. He smiled. We went our separate ways." She let out a slow breath. "The thing is, I knew right away what he *meant*. He was saying it was no big deal, what happened in the third quarter. It was just a stupid Pyramid, you know? I mean, he's just a kid, Mr. Stern. But it meant the world to me. It almost made me *cry*."

Missy eased back into her seat. Then she reached down, lifted her case — I had forgotten all about the case — and placed it on the table. It was covered with words and images cut from the pages of glossy magazines — images of flowers and men's flexing bodies and a pair of women's lips; words like "obsession" and "colors" and "boy." Across the middle, like a ransom note, block letters of varying color, height, and width spelled out, "Missy's Stuff." Looking at this box, it occurred to me: Anne was right. She was just a kid.

Missy unsnapped two silver clasps, flipped open the box. She reached in, withdrew the arrow — two-thirds of an arrow, really; the feathery end had broken off — and held it out to me. "I want you to have this."

"No." I held up my palm.

"I've thought a lot about this. I feel so powerless sometimes. Like there's nothing I can do."

"You keep it, Missy. I don't want it."

The lines in her face asserted themselves with tension. "*Please,* Mr. Stern. It would make me feel better."

I huffed and reached out. I grabbed the arrow. I don't know if I expected to feel some thrumming pulse, some physical connection to the son that I had lost. But I didn't. I felt nothing. A big fat shiny zip. It was just a broken dowel with a sharp rubber tip.

As soon as I took the arrow, though, Missy's eyes welled with tears. She brought a hand up in front of her face and waved it three, four times quickly. "Whew," she said. "I promised myself I wouldn't do this." She sucked in a breath and let it out with some tenor behind it.

I dug my elbows into the table, held the arrow in my fist, and cupped my palm over the point. I imagined running the arrow through her neck. I saw blood spattering into her fake blond hair, racing down the slick surface of her vest. I saw Missy clutch at her throat, her face plastered with surprise.

"Mr. Stern? Are you okay?" She pressed a tear off her cheek. "You're bleeding."

I sat on a vinyl bench at Mitch's Diner across from Missy Jones, the girl who killed my son.

Innkeeping

I wasn't looking for a new father when Tweedy walked into the bar. I was on all fours looking for a bicentennial quarter. I'd been mopping up when I banged the mahogany, knocking off a quarter left as tip. The coin rolled under the rail, and I couldn't reach it. When I stood, he was sitting there on a stool in front of me as if conjured from thin air.

It was the day after Christmas, three years after Dad died—I was on winter break from high school—and Mom and I were working to save the inn, though she already feared we wouldn't make it through to spring. Technically, I wasn't supposed to be behind the bar, since I was only fifteen. But Friendship Cove, New Jersey, was a beach town. In December, it was so empty we turned all the stoplights on the boulevard to flashing yellow and bumped up the speed limit to forty.

"What can I get you?" I said.

"You run this place?" He spoke with a British accent that seemed fake, and he wore a heavy tweed overcoat. He could have been Alcohol Beverage Control, but that was unlikely. ABC blended. Still, I didn't want to take any chances.

"I'm the innkeeper's son."

He considered this. "I'll have a Jameson."

"Rocks?"

He nodded. I dug a tumbler into the ice pit, pulled the green bottle from the rail, and poured him a shot. He was potbellied, maybe five-foot-six, with a kinky hive of brownish-gray hairs that pointed aggressively to his right; a brown vest strained at its buttons over a shirt with a large white collar. He put his elbows up on the bar and threaded his fingers — slender, hairless, and pink.

"Three bucks."

He reached into his front pocket and pulled out a silver money clip pinching a thick wad of bright bills. Peeled a crisp twenty and slid it across the bar, leaving it in the beer gutter. His eyes were a soft, cool blue, like Bombay Sapphire. "What's left is yours," he said, smiling.

I looked at it. "I'll make change."

"There's no need." He lifted the glass to his nose, sniffed deeply, then took a sip, closing his eyes.

I drew out the change and slipped the bills into my pocket, watching him. He put the tumbler down on the mahogany, then picked up his cocktail napkin and held it with two hands, tilting it so the dim overhead light caught the gold embossed schooner and the script words: "Oceanside Inn."

That's when Mom came in from the lobby entrance. "I'm running out." She walked briskly across the seating area to the front door. "Back in an hour."

"I'll hold down the fort," I said, before the door eased shut.

I opened the dishwasher at the far end of the bar and started unloading the few pint glasses we'd used the night before.

"Pardon me," the man said, leaning in toward the rail.

"Yeah?"

"That woman. She works here?"

"Who?"

"The woman who just left."

"That 'woman' is my mother."

"I meant nothing by it. It's just that I think I recognize her. I've stayed here before. Maybe ten years ago."

"Mom and Dad bought the place *six* years ago," I said. "It couldn't have been her."

He nodded, cupping his glass. "Your father," he said, "is one lucky chap."

When Mom returned, Tweedy was sitting on the porch swing looking at the thin reeds guarding the dune tops. I puttered behind the counter, punching random numbers into a calculator. Mom handed me a lumber receipt to record in the expense log. In the muted light glancing off the dunes, she looked pale and haggard, too old. She had a permanent dimple over her nose where her brow furrowed and deep creases at the corners of her lips. Her hair couldn't really be called reddish-brown any more. It was mainly gray now, with a few plucky strands of red hanging on for dear life. The side door chimes had announced Mom's arrival, and a moment later, Tweedy walked in.

"Mrs. Taft," he said.

"Yes?"

"The inn looks lovely. It's everything I remember."

Since taking over the inn, Mom had stopped smiling spontaneously. Instead, she drew from a catalog of smiles I'd come to know so well I'd numbered them, just to pass the time. On this occasion, she flashed Innkeeper Smile #7, "The Check-In": lips together, slightly turned up at the corners, eyes wide and inviting.

"How can I help you?" Mom said.

"Dr. Richard Thatcher," he said. "I'd like your best room, with a view of the ocean. For a month."

Mom arched her eyebrows. "A month?"

"I'm afraid so, yes."

She glanced at the reservations log. There were three names listed for arrival that week — two of them fakes. *Harvey Nardy* — a locals' bar at the northern tip of the island that Dad had liked to frequent. And *Count Perasto*—a legendary island shipwreck. "Stacking the log" was a trick I'd suggested, which mom'd instantly liked. The idea was, when potential guests glanced at it, they'd think there were other guests. People wanted what other people wanted, and they wanted a certain critical mass when they stayed at a bed & breakfast. They didn't want to think of the place as empty.

"It's $500 a *week*, Dr. Thatcher. And that's the off-season rate. There's really not much I can do—"

"Of course," he said, pulling the money clip from his front pocket, thumbing out five one hundred–dollar bills.

"Well, Dr. Thatcher," she said, reaching out for the cash, "welcome to the Oceanside Inn. The Melville Room should be just what you're after. A suite with a kitchenette and two fireplaces. Penthouse with balcony. Top floor, all to yourself. On a clear day, you can look out at the ocean and see the curvature of the earth."

She followed this with Innkeeper Smile #9, "The Curve of the Earth": lips parted, one eyebrow raised to suggest a tease.

"The evidence I've been searching for!" Tweedy said. "I'll take it!"

Mom launched into her perfunctory speech: oldest Victorian house on the island, destroyed in the hurricane of '46, rebuilt two years later. Twelve distinct guest suites, each named after a famous writer. Meeting place of the Friendship Cove Writers' Colony. Peter Benchley wrote the last chapters of *Jaws* in a fit of inspiration in the Homer Room. Breakfast orders at the front desk by eight P.M.; breakfast served at eight A.M., sharp. But there was something more upbeat in her cadence. Maybe because it was the first time since the summer she'd delivered that speech for a full-price walk-up.

"So," she said, "you said you've stayed here before?"

"A long time ago." Tweedy's eyes traced the crenelated molding that ran along the top of the wall like a castle battlement. "Ten years. It was called something else. The Sandy something."

"Sandy Bay," Mom said. "I was a clerk back then."

I stared hard at the calculator window as if looking for something I'd lost.

"Of course!" Tweedy said. "I knew you looked familiar!"

Mom blinked at her shoes. "It was a *long* time ago," she said.

"Anyway, it's up the stairs, three levels, far as you can go. My son, Will, will show you the way. If there's anything you need, Dr. Thatcher, please don't hesitate to call on us. If we're not here, we're at the cottage: out the door, up the path to the left."

"Richard," he said. "Please, call me 'Richard.'"

"Richard then. I'm Andrea."

Tweedy held his hand across the desk. When Mom took it, he reached out with his other hand and covered her hand with his. Then she smiled with her full face, relaxing her cheeks, muting her wrinkles. Her brown eyes were wide open and bright, and the freckles that swept across her nose seemed to pop, all at once.

It was a smile without a number. A smile I hadn't seen in years.

Dad had been a risk taker. Before purchasing the inn, he'd been a building contractor known for gambling on bay-front properties other contractors wouldn't touch. He built a house for us on a parcel of wetlands washed by the cool waters of the Great Bay. My bedroom window faced west, and in the spring, on school days, I awoke to the sound of tuna boats puttering through the channel, headed for Mudhole or the deep underwater cliffs along the continental shelf. On some mornings, the smell of baitfish stirred me even before my alarm clock. More than once, I awoke dreaming of giant squid.

Dad was a big, burly man, nearly six-foot-five, with thick, sturdy fingers, a crushing handshake, and tremendous strength in his arms and legs. He went for long ocean swims during jellyfish season, ignoring the red welts on his legs and back. He never complained about the cold, even in the bitter grip of winter when he used a sledgehammer to break apart the jagged ice that bit at our back door. Mom teased that he had been born without nerve endings, but it was a joke that seemed to scare her somehow.

He loved to sail. On clear days, he took Mom and me on long, sun-drenched cruises across Little Egg Harbor, sometimes putting his captain's hat on my head and letting me steer. But his true passion was "Storm Crashing." At the first sign of a thunderstorm, his buddies and he would race to their boats and head for the weather, hoping to catch the wind at its most ferocious. Even big boats like my father's keeled over well past forty-five degrees in the stiff winds leading green-bellied thunder clouds. Dad came back from Storm Crashing soaking wet, hair matted to his scalp, totally juiced on adrenaline. He'd prowl the house for an hour or more, searching for something to fix, or lift, or dismantle.

When Dad was out chasing thunder boomers, Mom and I waited for him in tense silence. Mom usually busied herself with work, or struggled to read, glancing out periodically at the darkening sky.

Though the whole idea of being out there before a thunderstorm terrified me, I always asked if I could go along. Dad seemed amenable, but Mom wouldn't hear of it. Don't become a thrill seeker like your father, she said. What she didn't understand, though, was that I didn't want to go for the rush. I wanted to go because if I was out there, I could watch over him. Keep him safe.

One day, Dad got a call from a friend about a line of storms firing toward the inlet. When he left for the boat, though, the sky above the inn was clear blue. I remember glancing up at the American flag on the pole in the parking lot and seeing it luff in a gentle breeze.

Dad rigged up his boat and headed south, straight for the storm's teeth. He ignored the small craft advisory that came in over the short band, and, according to the best guess of the Coast Guard, let the sail out all the way with the wind at his back. The boat would have been moving near its fastest, running downwind with the full force of the gale behind him. It would have been unnaturally quiet, with all the rigging pulling at the mast, the sail in a brilliant white bulge: nothing jangling, everything taut. It would have been then, under churning skies, when the boat edged into the storm front. The wind changed direction without warning and caught the boom in its most lethal position, hurling it across the deck in an uncontrolled jibe. It hit Dad's head, cracked his skull, and pitched him into the bay. They found him floating several hours later off the southern point of One House Island. From the coroner, we learned that Dad had drowned.

Sometimes, when things are going well for me — when I've just won some small victory maybe — that image comes at me, out of nowhere. I'll hear the rush of the wind as the boom swings over the deck. I'll see Dad standing at the wheel, rain peeling down his face, dripping from the brim of his hat. *Duck, Dad*! I want to shout. *DUCK*!

A few weeks after the accident, Mom and I went for a walk along the shore. The beach was deserted and the wind whipped up angry, swirling devils. Sand beat against my cheeks and brought tears to my eyes. The ocean was solid and colorless and seemed to roll in one immense swell.

"We're gonna get through this, Will," Mom said. "Together."

It was the first time she'd addressed our future—and until that moment, I hadn't known what to think. I was only twelve. I'd overheard adults saying things in hushed tones. Crazy things. *They'll have to sell the inn . . . Move in with her sister*. And nasty, callous things. *Something missing in his life . . . sent him out after storms*. Standing on the beach that day, Mom holding my two hands in hers, I could not have been more relieved.

And at first, it seemed we *would*—get through it. There'd been a small life insurance policy. Dad had friends in every sector of the business, and many of them donated their services for a while; we had a plumber, an electrician, and a heating and air man practically on call. Mom had kept the books when Dad was alive, and she turned to them with renewed purpose. She dubbed me the "utility innkeeper"; in my spare time, I did whatever needed doing, plugging up the gaps.

Gradually though, things changed. The inn aged. Exterior paint flaked. Framed black-and-white photos in reception of early island beach scenes tilted and stayed that way for weeks. A rust-colored water stain spread across the ceiling over the entrance foyer and dripped into a bucket. Worse, reservations were confused or mistaken. Once, a couple showed up for their anniversary—they'd called six months before—and we had no room for them. They had to turn around and go home. There was local speculation that the joy had gone out of it for Mom. That without Dad, she wasn't up to the task.

Within the year, a Holiday Inn opened just off the beach. They charged less for tacky rooms with mail-order prints above the beds, and they had a heated pool and mini-arcade with pinball. When we drove by the chain on the boulevard, Mom looked straight ahead, jaw clenched, doing her best not to notice the full parking lot or the beach towels flapping over balcony rails.

Still, though, she was determined. She took out a loan, and we hired Dad's former business partner to reroof and reshingle. We put ads in the national travel magazines and paid for an expanded listing in the B&B registry. Our third summer after Dad died, we had a nineteen-day stretch with no vacancy—the longest since our first season.

I believed we were on the cusp of turning things around when Tweedy walked into our lives. It was inconceivable to me that Mom would want another partner. The inn bound us together. It was all we had.

On the third day of Tweedy's stay, Sally Mitchell picked up a fish head and rubbed her eyes. This was unfortunate for Sally, but potentially disastrous for us. Sally was the six-year-old daughter of the writer Gregory Mitchell, who had recently won the Paris-James award for his war novel *Purple Heart* and whose choice of the inn as a place to vacation with his wife and daughter had been noted in the *New York Post* society column.

Sally found the fish head at the edge of the ocean where the tide had left it. After examining its empty eye sockets and reddish-pink gills, she dropped it on the sand and started shrieking.

She was still screaming when Mrs. Mitchell helped her over the dunes into the office. If Dad were alive, Mom would have handled the situation calmly, with grace. She would have known what to do. But as soon as Sally and Mrs. Mitchell walked in—the girl wailing, the mother's eyes flashing anger—Mom blanched, glancing nervously back toward the kitchen, as if she'd forgotten to turn off the oven.

"What happened?"

"Something's wrong with her eye." Mrs. Mitchell's voice was part panic, part pique. "She can't *see*."

"It hurts!" Sally screamed. "It *burns*!"

"What burns?" Mom said.

Mrs. Mitchell spoke calmly but firmly, enunciating every word:

"Sally was handling a fish head. I told her to put it down—but too late. She says she was *stung*. We need help."

"Stung by what?" Mom said. "It's the middle of winter. There's nothing out there to sting her."

"I really don't give a damn *what*," Mrs. Mitchell said. "Please, Mrs. Taft, she's in pain. *Do* something."

"There's nothing I can do if I don't know what bit her."

Sally let out a piercing wail.

"Oh, for Christ's sake, call an ambulance then!" Mrs. Mitchell said.

"Will," Tweedy said. "Call nine-one-one."

I hadn't noticed, but in the commotion, Tweedy had slipped into the office.

I went behind the desk and dialed as Tweedy bent to one knee. He put one of his bony hands on Sally's shoulder, and with the other, coaxed her tiny white palm away from her eye.

"There, there, let me see. What's your name?"

The girl's lips trembled, releasing a sob.

"Sally," Mrs. Mitchell said.

"Let me take a look, Sally," Tweedy said. "I'm a doctor. I'm going to fix your eye."

Sally's face was red and splotched, and her eyes were puffy. She resisted Tweedy, but her squirming was no match for him. Tweedy held her head with one hand and lifted her eyelid, ignoring her scream. "Scale," he said calmly. He scooped the girl up in two arms. "She's got a scale in her eye," he said to Mrs. Mitchell. "I'll flush it out."

He carried Sally to the washroom, filled the sink with warm water, and directed her to submerge her face, open her eye, and count to ten under the water. It was a quick ten count. When she lifted her face, she took in a fast breath, water running in streams down her neck, into her sweater. She blinked. Her expression was blank. She stared at Tweedy, astonished. "It's gone," she said. "It doesn't *hurt* anymore."

By the time the paramedics pulled into the lot, Sally was sitting in the dining room eating a cherry Popsicle and giggling at Tweedy's goofy faces. Mom explained the situation to the medics and apologized for calling them out. The world-class writer had returned from a walk and was sitting at the table next to his wife.

Mrs. Mitchell was talking furiously, recalling every detail, embellishing shamelessly.

When the Mitchells left, Mom walked over and stood in front of Tweedy. She put the back of her hand to her forehead. "Whew! I do declare," she said, in a faux-Southern accent. She wobbled on her feet, as if she were going to drop. It was her fainting act. And it was a good one, too. She could have been in pictures.

Tweedy, though, didn't catch on. He leapt off his chair and reached for her with both hands, fingers spread. Mom closed her eyes. And for some reason, she let herself fall backwards. She ended up in his arms.

———   ═══

We didn't see much of Tweedy the next day. I spotted him once up on the widow's walk, hands clamped to the wooden banister, looking out at the sea. He wore binoculars around his neck and brought them up periodically to view ocean liners, way out in the shipping lane. At three o'clock he went for a walk along the beach—south, toward the bird sanctuary.

On New Year's Eve, Mom hosted her customary get-together in the dining room for our half-dozen guests. That we had only one-third occupancy wasn't great, but it wasn't as bad as the year before—we'd had only two guests, and no party—and Mom was determined to make the best of it. She brought in the chef from The Shell, along with Mandy Mills, our best summer waitress, who circulated with trays of clams casino and shrimp cocktail. The guests drank champagne and mingled, complimenting Mom on the food and lovely ambiance. Mom was in her element.

Still, she seemed distant much of the night. She checked her watch and fussed over everyone, refilling their flutes. At one point, she asked me if I thought Dr. Thatcher might come. I shrugged. I was pretty pleased he hadn't already graced us with his presence. Just before midnight, though, he strode in from the office wearing his standard white collared shirt and brown vest. He stopped, looked around, saw Mom, and lifted a hand in greeting. She ran to him and struck up an instant conversation. They were sitting next to each other on the couch, shoulders touching, as the new year began, Mom leading everyone in "Auld Lang Syne."

The morning after New Year's Day, Mom said I should take advantage of the mild weather and work on the boardwalk. The wooden pathway led from the screened-in porch to the beach between round-topped dunes. My winter project was to replace the planks that had eroded and splintered. If Dad were alive, I would have relished the task—we would have done it together—but I'd been procrastinating.

I was down on one knee in the sand with a row of nails pointing out of my mouth when Tweedy came bounding off the steps, looking as dumb as a basset hound.

"Good morning, Will, Andrea," he said, saluting.

On the patio, Mom stopped sweeping and waved. "Good morning, Richard!"

"Glorious day," he said. "They don't make them any finer."

Mom smiled. "You must have some pull with the weatherman."

I'd heard her use this line a hundred times. Tweedy, though, seemed positively delighted by it. "Pull with the weatherman!" he said. "I'll have to remember that one!" Then, approaching me: "You look like you could use a hand, Will."

I took the nails out of my mouth and laid them on a board bubbling with sap. I could smell Tweedy's cologne. "No," I said. "I'm fine."

"Don't be silly. We can do this job in half the time if we do it together."

"Thank you, Dr. Thatcher, but I've got it covered."

"Really, Will. A bloke can go stir crazy if he's without honest work long enough. I'd love to help."

"Of course you can help, Richard," Mom said. "That's very kind of you. Will's behind." She turned to me. "Will, go get the other hammer, please."

"But, Mom. Dr. Thatcher's on vacation. I wouldn't want to trouble him."

She closed her mouth, shifting her jaw. Forced a smile. "This is not up for discussion, Will. Richard has made us a very kind offer. Get the hammer, please."

I walked along the side of the inn toward Dad's tool shed. As I rounded the corner, I heard a burst of Mom's laughter. When I knew I was out of sight, I kicked an explosion of sand at the shingles. Then I walked past the inn, around the dunes the long way to the cottage, got my bike, and just kept going.

By the time I returned, the light was edging out of the sky. Tweedy had plied off two dozen rotten planks and already laid half a dozen new ones. I slipped behind him, into the inn, to start setting up for dinner. Mom was already inside.

"Where where you?" she asked, her face tight.

"Arcade."

She nodded, without looking up from a table she was setting. "When I ask you to do something," she said, "I expect you'll do it."

"I didn't want him to help."

"I didn't ask what you wanted," she said.

She didn't say anything else. Just let the silence stand there between us. And over the next few minutes, it seemed to grow into something solid, a bulkhead wall. It wasn't until the first guests walked in that she looked up and smiled—"Welcome! Welcome!"—leading them to a table without skipping a beat.

Mom and Tweedy chatted every chance they got over the next few days. She mentioned some of the things she'd found out about him—that he was divorced, for instance, and that he was a vascular surgeon in Chicago with two daughters. If she found out other things, like why he'd shown up at the inn unannounced the day after Christmas, why he was staying for a month in the middle of winter, and why he paid for everything in cash, she kept those to herself.

The second weekend of his stay was busy. We had a couple of reservations and a few more walk-ups: a father taking his son fishing for ling and a Soho-based artist in the midst of a creative crisis. I didn't think much about Tweedy. The sudden rush even seemed to bring Mom back from la-la-land. We had a bed and breakfast to run.

By Monday morning, the inn had mostly cleared out. It was still dark when Mom and I left the cottage and wove between the dunes to the inn, the ocean reflecting a three-quarters moon. Mom put up the coffee and asked me to bring the *Philadelphia*

Inquirers up to the couples in Hemingway and Defoe, and also to Tweedy, but when I turned, newspapers in hand, he was standing there beside me.

"Good morning!" he said. He held a dog-eared copy of *Jaws*, one of the paperbacks we kept in the armoire in the breakfast nook.

"Good God, Richard!" Mom said. "What are you doing up?"

"Beach is beautiful this time of day. I took an early morning stroll."

That's what he said. But the dark depressions beneath his bloodshot eyes told a different story. By then, his pale skin had reddened with winter-burn; his hair was uncombed and frayed. His white collar, coffee-stained. Tweedy looked as though he hadn't slept in a week. Behind him, beyond the window, the first aquamarine tint of day crept into the sky above the dunes.

"We didn't get a breakfast order from you last night," Mom said. "What would you like?"

"Have you eaten?"

"Have *we* eaten?"

"You do eat, presumably."

"Well, no, I guess we haven't."

"Say no more. Breakfast will be served at half past the hour. Meet me in the breakfast nook. You too, Will."

"Richard, please," Mom said. "You don't need to do this."

"I insist!" he said. "You both worked very hard this weekend. And besides, cooking relaxes me."

Mom protested a bit more, but she was smiling, relishing the attention. Finally, she looked at me, shrugged, and then glanced back at Tweedy. "I haven't had breakfast made for *me* in years."

"A British inversion," he said, smiling. Then he promptly disappeared into the kitchen.

Mom shook her head, disbelieving. I took the newspapers, walked them up to the guest rooms, and then did the license plate run, making sure the cars in the lot were registered. At 6:30 sharp, Mom found me dragging a wet rag across the bar. "Soup's on," she said.

"I'm not hungry."

"Have a cup of coffee," she said. "Richard went through all this trouble."

"I'm behind."

"Will . . ." she said, folding her arms. "You've got special dispensation from the boss. Come on."

I could see there was no point in arguing, and besides, I'd caught a whiff of whatever it was Tweedy was concocting, and my stomach hadn't stopped rumbling since. I followed her into the breakfast nook. We sat at a three-top covered with a freshly laundered tablecloth, sunflower yellow. Tweedy emerged from the kitchen, placed a round globe oil candle on the table, and lit it with a flourish, sending his shadow skittering to the ceiling. "Voilà!"

He brought out coffee first. Then fresh squeezed orange juice and hot oven rolls with black raspberry jam. While we drank coffee, the color came suddenly into things outside: I saw it first as a red stripe on an American flag one beach south.

When we were ready, Tweedy brought out three plates, balanced on his arm. Each held a steaming Swiss cheese and tomato omelet, browned potatoes with fried onions, and thick slabs of cinnamon camp toast. He refilled the coffee.

"Can I get anyone anything?"

"Richard, sit, please!" Mom said. "Join us!"

He smiled, did as he was told.

Mom and Tweedy spoke about the weekend and the guests. Tweedy enjoyed talking with Mako, the Soho artist. She had promised to send him a catalog of her work. Mom told Tweedy about the wide-eyed young couple who had checked in as Mr. and Mrs. Everson. At one point, when Mom called to the woman and addressed her as "Mrs. Everson," though, she didn't respond. Mom guessed that they were not really married and couldn't understand why they'd go through the trouble of the ruse.

"Sometimes, it's just easier to pretend you're someone you're not," Tweedy said, bringing his napkin to the corner of his lip.

I looked at Mom. It was an incredible thing to say. Pretend you're someone you're not? But it didn't even register.

"And the oddest thing," she said. "The 'Defoe Room' sign is missing. I think they must've taken it."

"Off the *door*?" Tweedy asked.

Mom nodded. "It's happened once or twice before. I guess people want keepsakes."

"You'll send them a letter, I hope. Asking for it back."

"Oh no," Mom said. "They're just kids. A local artist paints those. I'll just commission another."

"You should send them a bill, at the very least," he said, holding her gaze.

"They meant no harm."

"All the same."

For a few seconds, the only sound was the *tinking* of forks on china. Then Tweedy looked at me and said, "You know, Will, I've got a daughter about your age. Tracy. She's fourteen. She'd love it here. These beaches have character. Maybe I'll bring her next time. You could show her around."

"Not much to show," I said. "What you see is what you get."

"I bet you could show her a thing or two." Tweedy smiled. "She's going to be a real beauty one day. A true-blue heartbreaker. Big blue eyes and curly dark hair. Smart as a devil."

"She sounds darling," Mom said.

"She is. My younger one, too. All a father could wish for."

"This one's pretty special too." Mom jerked a thumb in my direction. "I couldn't run this place without him."

"I can see that," Tweedy said.

Silence snuck up on us again. *Tink . . . tink . . . tink.*

Tweedy forked a triangle of egg, started chewing. "So, Will," he said, "what do you want to be when you grow up?"

A half-chewed piece of food flew from his mouth and landed on the tablecloth next to my plate. Mom put her fork down and looked over at me as if Tweedy had just come up with the most fascinating question on earth. With the morning sky behind her and the candlelight showing the freckles under her eyes, she seemed young and fresh and more alive than I'd seen her in years. But I got no joy from seeing her this way. I was hard-pressed to remember a single victory we hadn't shared together: a no-vacancy sign swinging in the breeze before Memorial Day; a good write-up in a Philadelphia paper; a kind word from a well-known poet. These things had always been ours, together.

"Well, Will?" Mom said.

Tweedy flashed me a smile, rigid as a U-bracket.

"I am grown up," I said. "I'm an innkeeper."

Another week went by, and Tweedy seemed to turn up with Mom all over the place. They'd started taking long walks along the beach. I got back from the arcade one afternoon and saw them standing on the widow's walk, leaning against the banister. The wind from the south tossed Mom's hair in her face, but she hardly seemed bothered. A few days later, I walked into the office and heard Mom's laughter, coming from the porch. I thought she was talking on the phone to Aunt Suzie or her girlfriend Jeanne, but then I heard his voice. I threw open the door and went out, and there they were, swinging together on the bench Dad and I had hung, Mom leaning on Tweedy's shoulder. She sat up with a start and slid away, adjusting her dress under her hips.

Whenever Mom and I were alone, she would wait for a quiet lull and then bring Tweedy up as though the thought of him had just occurred to her. Her voice always sounded rehearsed: "He's very good around the inn, Will, don't you think?" "He really is quite the handyman." "He's fond of you, Will. You should give him a chance."

The more she mentioned him, the more comfort I took from Sunday, January 24—his scheduled departure. Whenever Mom and Tweedy went on one of their beach walks, I'd flip open the gray metal box where we kept the reservation cards and reread the date, just to settle my stomach.

I picked up where Tweedy'd left off on the boardwalk: school started again the day after Tweedy left, and Mom said if I didn't get it done by then, it wouldn't be finished 'til spring. One morning, while banging in a two-by-four, I watched Tweedy lean against his banister, gripping the aging wood. It occurred to me that we hadn't replaced that railing in years. I could easily pull out a few nails along the base, loosening the railing just enough so that, if Tweedy pressed his weight against it, he'd topple.

I imagined the medics returning. Only, this time, leaving with Tweedy on a stretcher.

That evening, while setting up the bar for happy hour, I heard Tweedy talking to Mom in the lobby. I caught his eye through the doorway, and he gave me a halfhearted smile. A minute later, through the bar window, I saw him driving off the parking lot. The direct way from the lobby to the lot was through the bar, but he'd taken the trouble to go out the service door, around the shed, all the way around the inn.

I'd sensed it before, and now there was no denying it: Tweedy was avoiding me. There was something he didn't want me to know.

"What's up with Tweedy?"

Mom and I sat together behind the front desk. I punched random numbers into the calculator.

"Who?"

"Tweedy." I divided something by something else. "That doctor guy."

"Dr. Thatcher?" she said. "Will, that's not nice. What's gotten into you? Where're your manners?"

"I just don't like the mystery, that's all."

"What mystery?"

"Don't you think it's strange? I mean the guy's supposed to be on vacation, and he's fixing the boardwalk and making us breakfast. Turning up all over the place in the nick of time to save the day."

"Will!" she hissed, her voice low, looking over her shoulder toward the screened-in porch where Tweedy liked to read. "I've had just about *enough*. You know better."

"You heard him. Sometimes it's easier to pretend you're someone you're not? If you ask me, you shouldn't be telling him your secrets. He's probably running from something. I don't know what. Maybe the law."

She swiveled her chair so she could look at me, then reached and held me at the wrist, compelling me to glance up from my calculations, fire in her eyes.

"Dr. Thatcher's business is none of yours."

Then she stood, put on her jacket, and walked onto the porch, letting the wooden screen slam behind her.

There came a day during the fourth week of Tweedy's stay that I found myself fixing a leaky shower in the Fitzgerald bathroom, directly below the Melville Room. By a quirk of acoustics, voices from the Melville Room could sometimes travel into the Fitzgerald bathroom through a vent above the showerhead. To hear them, you needed to stand on the edge of the tub, crane your ear to the vent, and hang on to the shower pipe where it came out of the wall. The transmission quality varied depending on the pitch of the speaker and the direction of the wind. Sometimes, you couldn't hear a thing.

Maybe that's why I was taking my time, lingering near the vent. It wasn't something I'd planned in advance. It just happened that as I was removing the showerhead, Tweedy's voice came to me so clearly we could have been in the same room.

"I can't do it," he said.

I froze. Closed my eyes, cocked my ear to the vent.

"I'm telling you," he said, after a moment. "I just can't." His voice was strained, desperate. "I'm a goddamned alcoholic, that's why."

My heart pounded. I pressed in toward the vent.

"For Christ's sake, I'm in trouble here."

He went on speaking, but a Coast Guard helicopter passed up the coastline and I lost his voice. When things quieted down, I held my breath. The only sounds were the wind through the window screen and the blood surging in my ears.

I stepped off the edge of the tub, felt my jaw hinge open. Tweedy was a *drunk*. All his heroics, an act. Everything he'd told Mom was a barefaced lie.

Still, I might not have done anything. But later that night, as we walked back to the cottage together, Mom told me Tweedy had invited her to the Melville Room for a Chicago-style home-cooked meal. "A real live date," she'd said. "How about me, Will?" She accepted for Friday night, two days before Tweedy's departure.

The next morning, as I finished stacking firewood, I heard music coming from the laundry room. I walked through the kitchen, into the service hallway, and saw her through the open door. Mom stood, facing me with her eyes closed, holding one of Tweedy's collared shirts to her nose. As I watched, she inhaled, lost in the fabric, taking him in.

My knees jellied. I staggered backwards, through the hall, stumbling into the office. Leaning across the counter, I grabbed the metal box and flipped it open, thumbing through the cards until I found Tweedy's.

I noticed the pink bits right away. The checkout date had been erased.

I waited until three-thirty on Friday, when Tweedy's figure had disappeared in the shifting sands to the south. I took the master key from the front desk, padded quietly up the stairwell, and let myself into the Melville Room, duster in hand. There was a cardboard box of linguine and a small can of tomato paste on the counter, next to an onion, a green pepper, and a few cloves of garlic. I ran the duster over top of a half-dozen ripe tomatoes on the butcher's block. In the refrigerator, I found a stick of butter, a half-gallon of milk, and an empty pickle jar. I looked through all the cabinets, working quickly. Checked the closet, and then the bathroom, under the sink. I swiped at the faucet with my duster, glancing over my shoulder.

He had to have his booze somewhere. Alcoholics *drank*, and he hadn't been in the bar since that first night. It occurred to me maybe he kept a secret stash in his car, or on the beach, hidden under planks of driftwood between dunes. I considered just telling Mom what I knew—she'd never start up with a drunk, not with all we had on the line—but in her current state, she wouldn't believe me. I had to let her see for herself.

Downstairs, I took a brand new Jameson bottle from under the bar. Tied a red ribbon around the bottle's neck, then stepped back to admire my work. The bow was slightly askew. It looked like a drunken Englishman's gaudy bow tie.

That night, Mom and I left the inn at five so she could start getting ready. "I feel like I'm sixteen again," she said, as we walked between the dunes. In her bedroom, she tried on three outfits, each with a different pair of pumps. She stood in front of her mirror and turned on the ball of her foot. Looked over her shoulder to view herself from a different angle. Finally, she settled on a black wool dress, sleeveless, boatneck—a number that showed off her figure—with a cashmere stole and a pair of black boots. She held up four necklaces before choosing a simple choker of pearls. I looked at her reflection in the mirror as she picked lint off her hip and knew Dad was right—what he'd sometimes say when she was checking in a guest or taking a breakfast order and could only blush in defense: There was no more beautiful woman in the world.

"How do I look?" Mom said.

I put a thumb up.

"Okay, then," she said, moving toward the door. "Wish me luck."

"Mom," I said, finding my voice. "I thought you might want to give Richard something. A gift." I stepped into the hall, retrieved the Jameson bottle I'd left next to the door, and presented it, bow first. "It's his favorite."

Mom cocked a stern eye at me. "Whiskey?"

"Irish whiskey," I said. "He ordered it at the bar, once."

"He's been to the bar?"

I nodded. "His first day here."

She let out a breath between rounded lips. Then she wrapped her arms around me and squeezed. She held on for a moment. I felt a hot tear on my neck. "Thank you, Will," she said, pulling away. "I couldn't ask for a better son."

———

I figured Mom would walk in and give him the bottle, suggesting they warm up with a little nip. Tweedy shouldn't have a drink—he knows this. Maybe he even declines. But Mom's insistent, charming; the familiar green bottle, tempting. He imagines how it will taste; the feeling of warmth that will ease out to his fingertips. He doesn't *need* the drink. He's in control. And, after all, he doesn't want to be rude about it—Andrea has brought this over as a *gift*. Besides, he's nervous. One drink won't kill him, just loosen him up.

Only, as it turns out, it's the best tasting drink he's ever had, and before Mom can finish her first, he pours another generous serving over *tinking* cubes. And then another, and another after that. Before long, he's operating under a different set of assumptions. The rules of decorum spin as fast as the room. And suddenly his pink hands are on her, groping, pushing her roughly against the bed, working clumsily at her zipper. She protests, but he pins her against the duvet. And then it's my turn to save the day.

Over dinner, Tweedy chattered incessantly. He talked about his practice and his girls. The Art Institute of Chicago and Wrigley Field and the Taste. The price of real estate on the Gold Coast. He asked Mom open-ended questions—*Did you ever think you'd become an innkeeper? Did you ever want to do anything else? Do you like the sauce?*—and then jumped in, excitedly, often before she could fully answer.

When they finished, Mom offered to clear—it was still hard for her to get out of innkeeper mode—but Tweedy stopped her. My neck muscles were cramping, and my fingers were sore from hanging on to the showerhead. Every so often, I had to shake them out and switch hands, then recontort, pressing in toward the vent.

That's when Tweedy said, "Can I get you something to drink? A double shot of Irish whiskey, perhaps?"

There was a moment of hesitation, and something unsettling stirred in me, a sudden pang of worry. *This might actually work*, I thought. And my pulse fired. *What if she gets hurt?* I considered bursting into the Melville Room and putting a stop to it. Confessing everything in a rush of words. But then I remembered Tweedy's voice—*I'm a goddamned alcoholic*—and my anger flared. I gripped the showerhead, turned my ear to the vent, held my breath.

"How's it going?" Mom said. From the clarity of their voices, I pictured them sitting at opposite ends of the sofa, vent hovering between them on the wall.

"Hellish, actually. I have about five minutes a day when I don't think about it. If I'm lucky. There are times I'd give my unborn child for a good, stiff drink."

I clasped the steel pipe, heart pounding.

"I'm sorry, Richard."

"My therapist says it's to be expected. This is how it goes."

"Small consolation, I bet."

"No, it's helpful remembering I'm not the first."

"Is there anything else I can do?"

"She says the key . . ." Tweedy's voice cut sharply. For a moment, all I heard was the steady rumble of the furnace three floors below. Something cold surged through me, and my arms felt weak. Mom knew? She knew and she didn't tell me? She knew and she didn't *dump* him? I craned my neck, tilting my ear this way and that until I caught her voice again, faint, in midsentence: ". . . gave me a bottle of Jameson to bring to you tonight, as a gift."

"You're kidding."

"I'm not. He wrapped a bow around the neck." She laughed. "He remembered that you ordered it at the bar that first day."

"I daresay that's thoughtful of him."

"I thought so, too."

"Perhaps I'm *not* the devil incarnate."

"I told you. Tincture of time."

"Have you told him about us?"

"There's no rush," Mom said. "We can tell him together. When you're ready."

A longer pause. Was he inching toward her on the sofa? Resting a hand on her knee? "Andrea," Tweedy said, finally. "Did anyone ever tell you how lovely you are?"

"Tell me again."

Silence. And this time, the silence held. From the timbre of the wind in the duct, though, I knew that I was still getting clear reception from the Melville Room. At first, I thought maybe Tweedy was just tongue-tied. But as the quiet swelled, reality slapped me in the face like a renegade wave.

I released the pipe and swiveled—it was instinct: get up to the Melville Room and tear down the goddamned door. Only, my foot slipped off the tub. I fell backwards, arms flailing, body twisting away. And for one brief moment, I was floating on air.

I'm on a bed. Above the chest, a framed photograph of Robert Redford and Mia Farrow, Redford wearing the white cap, Farrow with the peach-striped cartwheel hat. It's *The Great Gatsby* film poster. I'm in the Fitzgerald Room. Off to the left, an L of white light escapes from under the bathroom door. I fell. Mom sits on the bed to my left. Tweedy stands before me. The back of my head throbs. I fell and hit my head.

"Will!" Mom grabbed my hand. "Are you okay?"

I rubbed at a welt on my head, wincing. "I don't know," I said. "I think so."

Tweedy said, "Do you know where you are?"

I nodded. Spying on Mom and Tweedy. "The Fitzgerald Room."

"That's good. What's your name?"

"Will," I said. "Taft."

"Good, good." He reached up and held my eyelid open, shining a penlight into my iris. Keys jangled from the light. He directed the beam across the bridge of my nose into my other eye. "Eyes dilating and constricting."

Mom gripped my hand. "That's good?"

He nodded. "Stick out your tongue, Will. Very good."

"Should we take him to the clinic?"

"How do you feel, Will?"

"Like I hit my head."

Tweedy laughed. Ran a finger through my hair, separating strands, exploring the edges of a swelling knot. "Concussion, most likely," Tweedy announced. "He'll have one hell of a goose egg, but he should be fine."

"Thank God," Mom said.

And I suddenly felt tired, so tired, as if I'd just spent my very last stores of energy. I wanted to get away, fast. Before the questions started.

"I didn't mean to interrupt your . . . interrupt dinner," I said, standing. "I should go."

"Not so fast, Will," Tweedy reached out and put a hand on my shoulder. "Why don't you come upstairs and join us for a while? I was just about to put up some tea."

"Oh, no, no," I said. "Really, I don't want to bother you."

"It's no bother," Tweedy said. "You got a good knock on the head. You seem fine, but I'd like to watch you for a bit to make sure." His hand fell to his side. "Doctor's orders."

The dinner plates were still on the table. A pie sat uncut, cooling in a tin on the stovetop. Twin candles flickered with a salty beach breeze from under a lifted window sash. A small fire jitterbugged in the hearth, shooting streamers of gray smoke up behind red-painted bricks.

I sat on the couch next to Mom. At the stove, Tweedy filled three ceramic mugs with boiled water from a kettle, then brought them out on a tray — *peppermint tea . . . it will help settle him down,* he'd said — and sat on the plush armchair next to the hearth, cradling his cup with two hands.

"What the devil were you doing down there, anyway, Will?" He said, lifting his cup and sipping his tea, eyebrow arched.

I tensed. My ride was finally over. Mom knew *exactly* what I was doing in the Fitzgerald bathroom. I prepared for her disappointment like a blow.

"I asked him to fix the showerhead," she said. "Damn thing's been leaking on us for a month."

I looked up at Mom, heart skittering like a minnow in a tide pool. She held my gaze, and I wasn't quite sure what to make of it all until she smiled — lips nearly-but-not-quite together, brow relaxed, eyes kind and reassuring, ending with a subtle head dip. It was one of the originals, though it hadn't passed between us in a long time. Innkeeper Smile #3: "I Got Your Back."

"On a Friday night?"

"We've got guests arriving in the morning," she said. "It was now or never."

"Wow, Will," Tweedy said. "You're a tireless worker."

Mom reached out, found my hand, intertwined our fingers, and raised our doubled fist in the air. I rested my head on her shoulder, letting my hand fall to her lap. I smelled her perfume. Felt the prickle of wool against my cheek.

Their voices were low. Mom asked again about my head. Tweedy told her she should wake me every hour or so overnight. Make sure I respond normally. But he suspected I was going to be fine. By the time school started Monday, I'd be good as new.

I don't know how long we stayed that way. Their conversation meandered. I listened to the faint, rhythmic thudding of the ocean against the shore, the wash of water back to sea. The only marker of time was the joints and joists of the inn, creaking around us. At some point, I heard Mom say, "It's getting late, we should really be going."

"Oh, Andrea," Tweedy said, "you can't leave before a slice of deep-dish Chicago apple pie. It's legendary!"

"You stay, Mom," I said, standing. "I'm going."

"But . . . your head."

"I'm feeling better," I said. "You heard Dr. Thatcher. I'm okay."

"You could take a piece for the road, Will," Tweedy said.

"Thanks," I said. "I'm just gonna hit the hay."

Mom leaned forward and looked up at me, an expression of concern on her face. "You sure, Will?"

"Yeah," I said, "I'll be fine, Mom."

We said our goodnights. Then I walked across the woven oval carpet and let myself out, pushing the door shut behind me, leaving the two of them there in the Melville Room, together.

The
Herald

The phone was ringing as Dale put his key into the lock, turned, shouldered the door open. He put down his leather attaché, hooked his keys on the wall beneath the hat mirror, and walked quickly across the living room, his cat, Pulitzer, threading herself recklessly between his ankles. He reached the phone and snatched the receiver after the sixth ring—a microsecond before his answering machine picked up.

"Hello?"

"Tapper! Sweet Jesus! Thank God you're home!"

It was Simmons, the managing editor, calling, Dale figured, with a question on his story. Dale had spent all morning and part of the afternoon on the piece, a feature about Frank Carnevale, an

84-year-old who'd hurled a perfect game at Lucky Lanes—oldest man to accomplish the feat in the storied history of the alley and one of only three octogenarians ever to do so in the county. Dale'd interviewed the manager of the lanes and the head of the New Jersey Bowling Association. The kicker, though, was an exclusive, hour-plus interview with Frank and his wife, Estelle, at their home that afternoon. Dale hadn't started with much—just a press release announcing results of league play, with Frank's age noted parenthetically. Kind of thing that—with most reporters—sails straight from the inbox to the trash. But in the end, he'd really come up with something. *Lucky Strikes!: Danville Senior Bowls Historic Perfect Game.* It was running lead Community, Klamasink edition, with a photo Dale'd snapped of Estelle admiring Frank admiring his trophy on the shelf.

Dale had filed just after three, then started calling the cop shops. He'd written a half-dozen briefs for the blotter and topped it off with a no-frills, eight-inch advance of a Patawah Junction Board of Ed meeting. Sent his last piece just after 5:30, a half hour after his day technically ended, then dragged himself out of the newsroom. He was tired. Days like today, it felt as if he'd swum a marathon.

"What's up, Mike?"

"I just got a call from Hawker. They found a body in the river, south of Landing Lane."

Dale took in a slow, deliberate breath, glancing up at the circular clock over his sofa. Six twenty-two.

Hawker was a *Herald Times* tipster—one of their most reliable. He sat around in his basement all day, in his boxers and one of an assortment of rock band tour T-shirts, assembling and disassembling computers, tinkering with the circuitry, all the while monitoring the police scanner. Hawker, for the most part, didn't miss.

"Is it Missing Mom?"

"So Hawker says," Simmons said. "No positive ID yet. But you gotta believe."

Dale's next question—the obvious question—would have been: *So why are you calling me?*

Missing Mom was Croyle's story. Her Celica had been found three days before in a small, unlined parking area for an Esquand

River State Park trail, tucked off a lonely, wooded stretch of Route 19 in Willamette. It was Croyle who broke the story, on a tip from a cop who owed him a favor for a Police Benevolent Association lead, beating their three major Central Jersey competitors plus the statewide *Leader* to the punch by a full day. He'd had an exclusive with the missing woman's boss at Two Left Feet—the last person to see her the evening she'd disappeared—who said she'd received a call at work that afternoon and, thereafter, seemed pensive, distracted. *She left without punching her timecard.*

Jessica Lynn Laurie, 33, had two daughters, Lana, 10, and Lizzy, 4, and lived with her husband, Kevin, 36, a bike mechanic, in a 1950s split-level in Willamette. The owner of the shoe store, where Jessica worked as an assistant manager, said she was one of the best employees he'd had in two decades in the business, hands down. *There's just something about her,* he said. *She makes every customer feel like a lifelong friend. Jess could sell open-toed pumps to an Eskimo.* She grew up at the Shore, but in the photos the police circulated, she had a foreign look—dark curls, hazel eyes, charmingly gap-toothed, vaguely Eastern European. Staring out from the pages of newspapers and "Missing" posters around town, she was a natural beauty, perplexing, distant, maybe a little bit lonely, the kind of girl you'd love just to stop her from looking so sad.

The morning after her car was discovered, with the rest of the media playing catch-up, Croyle presented himself at Jessica Lynn's house, took off his sunglasses, knocked on the door. "Kevin looked like he hadn't slept in a month," Croyle later told a rapt newsroom. "He had his daughter—the little one—stuck to his leg. Every time he moved, there she went, right with him."

Croyle introduced himself. Said he was sorry to bother him. Even sorrier about his wife. He was working on a follow-up, though, and wondered if Kevin might have any insights, information that could help shed light on her whereabouts, maybe get the public thinking in a new direction. Kevin listened, casting a wary eye on Croyle, keeping the closed screen door between them. When he finally spoke, he said he already told the cops everything he knew, which wasn't much, and, beyond that, what could he say?

Croyle understood. Hundred percent. Told him Willamette PD

was working twenty-four seven to find Jessica Lynn. "They're doing nothing else right now," Croyle said, holding out his card. "They're the best, most professional men and women I've come across. If anyone can find your wife, Mr. Laurie, it's them."

The guy cracked the door, reached out over his daughter's unwashed curls, and took the card. Croyle turned, starting down the steps.

"She cuts the kids' waffles into stars every morning," Kevin said, projecting his voice, steady and firm. "And she uses the cutout pieces to make *butterflies*. If she's in trouble—" He closed his eyes, bent his neck, put a hand on his daughter's head, then, seeming to find something inside, raised himself up. "She's the most resourceful woman I ever met. She'll come back to us. I know she will."

"My money's on her."

He pushed the screen out, held it open. "You want to come in?" he said. "I was just putting up some coffee . . ."

Jessica, it turned out, often went to the towpath if she was wrestling with something, stuck on that Tilt-a-Whirl in her head. She loved the serenity of the floodplain; the way it changed, season to season, day to day, depending on the angle of the sun. She loved how, if you were open to it, the forest and river could speak to you. The day she was trying to decide whether to keep the surprise baby that turned out to be Lizzy, the forest had produced—*voilà!*—a buck, doe, and two fawns, at first visible only by the barest white flick of a tail through repeating gray trees. When she was virtually immobilized over whether they should buy the split-level in Willamette—move out of the Gateway Apartments, where they'd lived for a decade—she'd seen a downy woodpecker, working intensely at the gray bark of an elm, carving out a home.

Inevitably, on her walks, she would meander down to the towpath, following the grade, absorbing the slope with her knees, noticing how the smell changed: from pine to marsh milkweed to river, which, she'd told Kevin once before, was absolutely unique, if you thought about it, because name one other thing on earth that smelled of death *and* life, both at the same time. There, miles from the nearest car or person or inhabited building, she might finally, for the first time in weeks, take a deep breath. Feel her head begin to clear. By the time she got home, she was on her way to working out whatever it was that'd sent her there in the first place.

'*She'll Come Back to Us*,' Croyle's four column, 52-point banner headline declared.

It was solid gold. Simmons, never prone to understatement, conjectured that it was possibly the single most read article in the ninety-year history of the *Herald Times*.

The morning that story broke, nearly forty-eight hours after she'd gone missing, the Willamette Police Chief held a press conference, announcing that they'd found her sneaker print in a naked clearing by the river, near the dock at the abandoned concrete plant, along with several matching strands of hair on the third-to-last plank of a dock.

What concerned them more, though, was evidence of Person B: larger, mud-stamped boot prints on the dock; and, behind several large cranberry bushes within view of the pier, flattened grass, crushed-out cigarettes, an empty liter of whiskey. A couple who'd been on the towpath trail that afternoon had come forward to say they'd seen a man on their way out of the woods. Tall, maybe six five, dressed in a poncho though it wasn't raining. Carrying twin black Hefty bags. When the woman said hello, he mumbled something unintelligible. Later, when they heard the news of a mom gone missing, they immediately thought of the man and called the police right away. The Chief circulated a composite sketch—Caucasian, wide face, chin like a lightbulb, eyes a notch too far apart; dark, slick hair swept from a center part—calling him a "person of substantial interest." Off the record, they hypothesized that there'd been a scuffle and she'd entered the water off the pier.

That afternoon, volunteers stood shoulder-to-shoulder, sweeping the floodplain in slow-moving lines. Police divers combed the river, searching for Missing Mom in the deepest pools and eddies.

Within a half hour of the Chief's press conference, TV crews from Secaucus had set up camp outside the Laurie house, Action News vans lining the street. Broadcast images showed the split-level, shades drawn over two front windows, attached garage shut, set back from the road behind a cordon of yellow police tape. The whole day, no one came out. Channels Two, Four, and Seven resorted to showing close-ups of a child's bike tipped over on the grass and a dying black-eyed Susan, nodding in a planter attached to an iron porch rail.

Thereafter, phone calls to the Laurie house were picked up by an answering machine, Jessica's voice eerily alive, even ebullient: *You've reached Grand Central Station! If you're calling for —* here, she passed the phone around, as each family member called out in turn, *Kevin! . . . Lana! . . . Lizzy! —or Jess! Leave a message! And, please, watch your step!*

Now, three days after the disappearance, they had a corpse in the river, just a mile from the abandoned concrete plant where the physical evidence had been discovered.

Sure, the body had surfaced near Landing Lane Bridge, which was Patawah—one of three Klamasink County, New Jersey, towns that made up Dale's beat. But this was Croyle's story. If the situation had been reversed, Dale would have expected Simmons to give it to him.

"Croyle filed a half hour ago," Simmons said, anticipating the question Dale was about to ask. "I can't get ahold of him. He could be in fucking Cheyenne for all I know. I need someone at the river, half hour ago."

"I'm on my way," Dale said. "I'll call you as soon as I know something."

He hung up the phone. Hung up the phone, and, yes, this was a big story. One of the biggest at the *Herald* in a long while. Interest was more intense than almost anything he'd ever seen. He hadn't eaten dinner—and just tea and Lorna Doones for lunch on a tray served by Estelle Carnevale—but, still: *His hands were shaking?* That didn't make much sense.

Dale was a pro. There were a few longer-serving columnists and editors at the newspaper and a sportswriter, Gene George, who'd covered the New Jersey Americans in the ABA, when their chief competition was the Minnesota Muskies and Pittsburgh Pipers. But at 47, Dale was the longest-serving news reporter on staff, with twenty-one years at the paper. He'd covered plenty of big stories in his day. The Danville pipeline explosion. The Third Base Sinkhole Disaster. Plenty.

It was 6:26—two and a half hours 'til final deadline—and, once he had the story, frankly, he could type it with his eyes closed, one-fingered. Standing in his living room, he was already composing the lead:

> *Authorities pulled the body of Jessica Lynn Laurie, 33, from*
> *a muddy stretch of the Esquand River in Patawah yesterday,*
> *three days after her car was found in a small roadside parking*
> *lot off Route 19 in Willamette.*

Really? he thought. *My hands are shaking?*

"Get a grip," he said, out loud, in the empty apartment, his voice echoing between hollow walls and bare parquet floor.

And, as if he'd called her—as if Getagrip was her name— Pulitzer stretched her tabby legs up on his khakis, showed him her claws, and meowed once, beckoning Dale to scratch behind her ears.

"Not now, Pulley. Breaking news."

The truth—if he was being honest with himself—was it'd been awhile since he'd written a major, all-edition lead on tight deadline. Was it two years already since the Wrong Way crash on Highway 3 that killed a family of five and a van driver for the disabled? Now that he thought of it, that was the summer of '86. *Three* years before. His beat for the past four years—Danville, Patawah, Patawah Junction—was quiet compared to some of the others in the *Herald*'s coverage area. Reliably nine-to-five, Monday-to-Friday. Coveted for just that reason.

All together, his towns had a population of 51,503. Willamette alone had more than 120,000 people. The 'Met, as the Slot called it, was a beat unto itself—one of the most demanding at the paper, with thirty homicides a year, six Superfund sites, and a community college located on a former military arsenal where, on Croyle's watch, a co-ed cutting through the woods en route to home ec one day had stepped on a live slab of World War II ordnance, losing her leg and half a hand. Dale's beat, while important—the *Herald* was widely distributed and well read in his three towns — just didn't tend to generate those kinds of stories.

Dale hurried into his bathroom, splashed cold water on his face, toweled dry. Straightening, he buttoned his top button and adjusted his tie in the mirror, sliding up and tightening the knot he'd finally loosened at his desk, just an hour before. In the galley kitchen, he found three-quarters of a Hershey's chocolate bar in the drawer next to the sink and a thin belt of coffee in the pot, left over from his morning brew. He poured the last of the sludge into a ceramic *Herald Times* mug—the one with the paper's tagline: *Central Jersey's Paper of Record*—slid it in the microwave, and nuked it for thirty seconds, scarfing down the chocolate. When the timer beeped, he pulled out the coffee and slugged it back—a bitter, scalding jolt. Then he walked out the other end of the kitchen into the foyer, grabbed his attaché—a gift from his parents, from his father's store, on his twentieth anniversary at the *Herald*—and reached for the door.

The phone rang again. Dale bolted across the living room, gaffing the receiver with a hooked hand, as if it were the broad back of a marlin. "Yeah?"

"What the hell are you still doing there, Dale?"

Dale rolled his eyes, hung up huffing out a breath—then whirled, knocking the end table with his attaché.

"'Night, Pulley," he said. "Don't wait up."

Dale loved the *Herald Times*. He loved the simple, light blue, Goudy Old Style font of the flag. He loved the half-inch green bar beneath it, confidently declaring "The Newspaper for Klamasink, Wayne, and United Counties," as if their competitors simply did not exist. And he loved the hard-edged tenacity of the news staff. They were paid less than the reporters at the *Leader*, and they got far less recognition, but they stayed later at council meetings and filed three stories a day instead of one, and they wrote about the towns they covered as if their readers' lives depended on it.

The *Herald* was the paper that had been delivered to his house, growing up in Klamasink Borough. He'd made the front page himself once, during his elementary school Halloween parade, dressed as a bum in his father's oversized slacks and suspenders, half-moons of his mother's mascara beneath his eyes. In his senior year of high school, he'd been named Herald Times Athlete of the Week for catching touchdown passes of fifty-three and twenty-seven yards in a football game against divisional rival Opal Creek.

His head shot had run over the caption *Tapper leads Falcons,* and for weeks thereafter, people he didn't know came up to him at Krauszer's and Dunkin' Donuts, offering congratulations.

Dale'd started stringing for the paper shortly after graduating college, while working full-time at his father's luggage shop. He took any assignment they gave him, no matter how short the notice, and he paid attention—never complaining when his leads were rewritten or his editors, pressing him on a point, asked him to call back a source after deadline. He watched for job postings on the newsroom bulletin board, waiting for the right opportunity. When the Upland Borough beat opened, Dale collected his very best clips in an envelope and walked them into the office of Abe Kesting, Editor-in-Chief, introducing himself as "the stringer who wrote *Turmoil in the Firehouse.*" Kesting had glared at him. *My meetings are by appointment.* Two weeks later, though, Dale had his first newspaper job. *You're just reckless enough to be good,* Kesting said.

Over his years at the paper, as other editors and reporters came and went, Dale'd developed a ritual. At the end of a reporter's first week, usually Friday after deadline, he'd take him or her for a drink at Sal's, three blocks from the newsroom at the bottom of the hill, in the Italian section of town. They'd sit at the bar or—if someone had a preference—one of the wooden booths along the wall, and Dale would drill down through newsroom legend and lore. He told them about the time capsule, buried beneath the composing room, with a copy of the first issue, printed in 1899: *River Fest Lights Up Esquand.* He told them about the time Bob Woodward stopped into the newsroom on his way back from an interview at the U.N., to use the fax. And he told them about John Derrick, the founder and ruthless first publisher, who, famously—the day the paperboys went on strike—went down to the plant, loaded up his Essex Super Six, and, over the next eight hours, hand-delivered every last copy of the newspaper himself. They'd run a picture of Derrick on the paper's seventy-fifth anniversary, smiling, cheek smudged with newsprint, holding up hands black as tar.

Spend time in the archives, Dale advised. Read the people who came before you. Figure out how we got where we are today. When you file, lead with a haymaker, sure, but never forget the story you're writing is a continuation of a story we've been telling for almost a hundred years. A prelude to the next hundred. Pour your whole self into every article, write it as if it were your last, but don't try to be Shakespeare, don't get too precious—Queen's English is for the Queen—and above all else, don't miss deadline. The paper has come out with bad articles and flowery articles and wrong articles, pompous articles and just plain boring articles, but never with *no* articles.

Remember, Dale said. Somebody, somewhere, is picking up the paper and reading about the death of a friend. Someone with a heavy burden is circling classifieds, looking for work. Sure, someone's reading the funnies on the crapper, and someone else has tossed sections A and B aside so they can get straight to the baseball box scores. But right this minute, someone with a cup of coffee is settling down to the paper at a kitchen table or diner counter or bus depot as if it were a long-lost friend, a lifeline.

At least, it'd always been this way for him.

Dale pulled onto the shoulder behind three police cars and the Captain's cruiser, lights flashing, next to a strip of grass adjacent to the woods. Through the windshield, he saw someone—was it Officer Grange?—sitting behind the wheel in the car in front of him. Officer Cody emerged from the forest, holding a plastic bag with a gloved hand. Cody spotted Dale, lifted his head in acknowledgment. Dale pushed open his door, slung his attaché over his shoulder, made his way down the berm.

"Officer Cody," he said.

"Dale."

"Big doings at Marker 22 today, huh?"

"You might say so."

"Is it her?"

"Who?"

"Missing Mom. Did you find her body?"

He shifted the evidence bag to his side, out of Dale's sight. "You'll have to talk to Cap, Dale." He tipped his head toward the woods. "You know the drill."

Dale nodded, shifting his jaw.

"Thanks, Officer," he said, walking across the grass, glass from broken beer bottles crunching under his feet. "Appreciate it."

He stepped into the woods where Cody had exited, and right away, the chill rose up in him. He could smell the river, brackish and muddy, even from there, and a cold dampness brushed his bones. *This is what she saw*, he thought. *This is what she smelled.* And he felt—for the first time since the Missing Mom story broke—not pride that the *Herald* had been so consistently ahead of the pack, but something much closer to the heart, some faint shred of the unholy terror that must have gripped Jessica Lynn Laurie as a man approached her and she realized, all at once, that she'd made a terrible mistake, setting out on the towpath alone at dusk; as she was dragged or carried or forced, wrenchingly, through these very woods in the dwindling twilight.

Dale shivered. The sound of the breeze in the treetops was so benign, so lovely, it gave him goose bumps.

He hurried forward, stepping over fallen, rotting logs, twigs snapping. He was only a few minutes in when he heard low voices, sifting up. He adjusted his bag on his shoulder, found a passable route, avoiding a nasty shelf of thorns and poison oak, and made for the Esquand on a wire. He could feel the water in the earth, sucking greedily at the soles of his loafers with each step.

"Poor sad sap sonofabitch," he heard, and, now, he ran—at one point nearly losing his shoe in the muck, shielding his eyes from the limber branches of saplings as they scratched his face and poked his arms. Up ahead, he could see the light of a clearing, where the barges used to stop, where a wire works once accepted giant rolls of raw, coiled steel. He could hear the river, turning circles around the boulders in the shallows beneath the bridge.

"Ho-lee," Captain Grimes said, looking up from the other side of a line of police tape. "It's Tarzan himself. Call in the elephants."

Detectives DeAngelo and LaValle were in the clearing, too, the three of them standing in a triangle.

And there on the ground—a few feet beyond the cops, legs akimbo, torso partially obscured by high reeds at the water's edge, and framed, almost idyllically, by the soaring green trusses of the bridge—was the reason he'd come.

Dale flipped open his bag, quick-found his camera, pulled it out by the strap, and—focusing on the dead body in the middle-distance, with the unloading platform of the old wire works to the left and the bridge balancing the shot in the upper right—he clicked the shutter.

"What the holy hell do you think you're doing, Dale?"

"Working, Captain." He snapped another shot. "What's it look like?"

"You'll not take another photograph, or that camera just might find its way into the Esquand. What the hell happened to you, for God's sake?"

Dale reached up and touched his cheekbone, where it stung. Pulled his hand away. A bright film of blood marked three middle fingers. "I'm fine," he said, then, dipping his head: "What happened to her?"

"I'd sure like to say, Dale." The Captain walked three-quarters of the way across the clearing, boots squeaking, and stopped, positioning himself directly between Dale and the stiff. "We're not releasing any information at this time, however. We might have something for you on this tomorrow. Or, we might not. Hard to say."

LaValle took notes on a copy press template. DeAngelo reached into his shirt pocket, took out a box of Reds, flipped open the top at LaValle, who shook his head.

Dale approached the tape, strung between a gnarled old sugar maple and a lean-to post, dropped his camera in the bag, pulled out his flip pad. "So it's a Jane then?"

Grimes smiled, slowly, jutting his chin out. "Nicely done, Tapper. Okay. Got me there. Good detective work. I'll give you that. It's a Jane."

"Is it her?"

"Who, her?"

"Missing Mom."

"'Missing Mom' has a name, Dale."

"Jessica Lynn Laurie. Is it her? Our sources say it's her."

"Do they now?"

Dale nodded. "Have you ID'd the body?"

"Investigation's pending. Wish I could help, Dale. You certainly look like you need it."

DeAngelo snorted out a smoky laugh. LaValle shook his head from side to side, lips pursed. Grimes smiled, flashing tar-stained teeth.

Grimes. He hadn't forgiven Dale for a series of articles he'd written ten months prior about Lieutenant MacLachy, a veteran on the force, who was taking free meals down at the Riverside Inn and in return providing protection. The owner of the joint would call MacLachy, late night, if something went down—fights, rambunctious under-agers, a car keyed in the parking lot—and he'd show up in plain clothes and handle everything, without filing a report. *Much ado about nothing*, Grimes had said at the time, pointing to MacLachy's unblemished, quarter-century of service. *Seasoned cop helping out a friend.* Maybe so. But it was also a clear violation of the department's conflict of interest policy, and when Dale's story was picked up by the AP in Trenton, the mayor forced the Chief to formally reprimand MacLachy, tarnishing his record, clouding his retirement.

Dale put a hand on the tape, felt the breeze moving through it.

"Now, if you'll excuse me," the Captain said, "we're kinda busy right at the moment . . ."

"Captain," Dale said. "I see you've got your hands full. Last thing you need is me here, gumming up the works. Can you just—tell me who found the body? I'll get out of your hair."

"Fisherman," he said, immediately. "Poor sad sap sonofabitch. Guy was looking for catfish and found a stiff. He's pretty shook up about the whole thing."

"Can you give me his name?"

He glanced over his shoulder. "Franky," he said. "What's the name of that Italian?"

LaValle looked down at his notes. "Moretti, Chief," he said. "Viggo Moretti."

"Can you spell it for me?"

"Like it sounds."

"Can I see the pink?"

"No, you can't see the pink, Dale. What was I, born yesterday?"

Cops, in the end, were like tackling dummies. You could push them, but only so far.

Dale glanced away. There was a stately magnolia tree on the far side of the clearing. If he could climb it, he could pop on his zoom lens and get a better shot of the body. Of the face. Captain looked across the clearing at the tree, then back at Dale. A tower of heavy white clouds moved over the cracked windows of the wire works.

"Will there be an autopsy?" Dale asked.

Something leapt across the Captain's brow. Anger, leavened with a dash of confusion. Blood drained from his cheeks, and he charged the rest of the way across the clearing, halting abruptly, raising himself up just on the other side of the curved tape, glowering at Dale with wolfish eyes. Dale could've counted the burst capillaries on Grimes's nostrils.

"We're sending the body to the County, soon as our work is finished," he said, calmly — gun, flashlight, handcuffs, and walkie-talkie steady at his hips. "Now, Dale, I'm gonna start counting. If you're half as smart as you think you are, you'll haul your ass out of here, before I get to ten."

He drove immediately to the Sunoco Station, pulled up alongside the pay phone. There was only one Moretti in Klamasink County. "Connect me, please," Dale said. He waited. *Come on. Come on!* After a dozen rings, he checked his watch — 7:37 — hung up, and dialed the newsroom. The phone rang once, twice, a third time.

"What!"

"It's Tapper, Mike," he said. "I just left the river. I saw the body."

"And?"

"It's a Jane. That's confirmed. They won't ID her, though . . ."

"You told him we're on deadline?"

Dale moved the receiver to his other ear, closed his eyes, pictured the scene again. He'd only gotten that first quick look at the body before Captain blocked his view. He was trained, though, not only to *look* at a scene, but to *see* it. And when he closed his eyes, there she was, each and every time. Something in her face, and the darkly matted curls.

". . . but, Mike, I'm pretty sure it's her. Missing Mom. I've got a lead. Don't give up on me just yet."

"Dale," Simmons said. "You've got eighty minutes to nail this thing shut."

"I know."

"Seventy-nine."

"I'm on it."

"Do you need help? I've got V-Ray right here. She can be there in a titmouse heartbeat."

"No, Mike, I'm good." Dale swatted at a firefly, crowding his airspace. "I've got it covered."

"Tell me: Who else was there?"

"Just me."

"Just you?"

A semi blew by on the highway, shuddering the phone booth, pulling a curl of roadside litter up over the hood. "Right. Looks like an exclusive on the body."

"Okay," Simmons said, after a moment. "I'm holding the lead. Go get it."

Dale stepped onto the planks leading to the river. He'd already tried the Sinktown Boathouse—the proprietor had never heard of a Viggo Moretti—and now, Dale had forty minutes, and he was no closer to paydirt. He walked between white-sided wooden buildings, under a covered walkway, then out on the dock. The marina wasn't very big—one central row, four piers running off on either side, like the tines of a clam rake. There were maybe twenty slips on each row, 150 boats total. Bowriders, sailboats, pontoons. A few Jet Skis. Out here, in the open air of the river, there was still some lavender light in the sky—but not much. A bass boat moved silently through the channel drawn by a lime-green bow light, charming an osprey above.

The wind had come up a little from earlier in the day, and the sounds were all nautical: a halyard clip, clinking against a mast; the strain of the lashing ropes on rising cleats; the river, lapping innocently at fiberglass hulls. One man worked on the deck of his sailboat, on the third pier to the left, and Dale started for him, planks creaking underfoot.

"I'm looking for a Viggo Moretti," Dale said. "Does he dock here?"

He raised his head above the gunwale. "Check inside," he said.

Dale turned, hurried back down the center dock.

There was a sign on the door, at the end of the covered walkway: "The Club—Private." Dale pushed down on an old iron thumb press, pulled the handle, stepped inside. The place was dark, lit only by flickering electric candle bulbs along the walls, and, above the doors, oval bulkhead lights. A waitress took an order from two men seated at a heavy wooden table that looked like it might have been pried from a shipwreck. Across the room, a man sat hunched over the bar, alone.

Dale approached, carefully, from behind. Put his bag down and took a seat at the bar, leaving one stool between them. Framed photos above the rail showed smiling men, standing on the dock, or in boats, fingers buried deep in the gills of river catfish, carp, and striped bass. The man glanced absently at Dale, settling onto his seat. Pale blue eyes, wide, tanned face, lustrous gray hair combed neatly, straight back, still wet from a shower. He cradled a tumbler of swirling bronze with two hands. On the cuff of his tailored dress shirt, rising and falling between angled, bird-wing brackets, was a monogram: *VCM*.

Dale held his breath. A man with a bowtie appeared from swinging kitchen doors, cut a path across the dining room, raised the bar-flip. "What can I get you?"

"Water," Dale said. "Slice of lemon, please."

"Better watch," the man on the stool said, speaking with a thick, old-country accent. "That stuff'll grow hair on your chest."

"Have to stay away from the good stuff," Dale said. "I'm working."

"Don't look like it."

Dale glanced over at a propeller clock on the wall. If he wasn't back in the office in a half hour, his story was a bust. "I'm a reporter," Dale said. "*Herald Times?*"

Now the man swiveled on his seat, appraising Dale from top to bottom to top. "Don't look like no reporter, either," he said.

"Yeah, well," Dale said. "You don't look like a fisherman."

He laughed. Lifted his snifter, took a slow sip.

"Dale Tapper," he said, holding out his hand.

"Viggo Christophe Moretti," he said, gripping with a hand like salted sandpaper. "I've been waiting for you. I know why you came."

Dale reached into his case, pulled out his pad. "I understand you had a tough day out on the river."

Moretti pursed his lips, nodding.

"I'm working on a story about that," Dale said. "I was hoping you could tell me what you saw."

"You gonna put my name in the paper?"

The waiter placed a tall glass of water on a coaster. Dale slipped the lemon off the rim, pressed juice over his cubes. "If it's okay."

Moretti dipped his chin. He might have been searching for something in his tumbler, except his eyes were closed. When he opened them, he was looking through his drink, not at it. "You ever been in the army, Mr. Reporter? Vietnam?"

Dale shook his head side to side. "My number didn't come up."

Moretti nodded. "I haven't seen a thing like that since the War."

"A thing like what?"

Moretti sighed, heavily, hunched over the bar. "Started like any day," he said. "Drifting the channel for striper. They start up again this week. Guy I know caught three at Milt's Point. Only, for me—" he slashed a finger across his throat, "*zero.*

"I change, from fish egg to worm. Catch a sucker. Not much. It was gettin' late, so I decided to try the bridge. Sometime, catfish are in the pools. Real active, late afternoon, early evening."

"I've seen them there," Dale said. "From the walkway, on the bridge."

"See? Yes. Catch? This is another story. I put my baits down. The fish, though—no interest. So I give up. Start working the shore—working my way back—using spoon, with chicken livers. Cast and reel. Cast and reel. I had just cast near some weeds, by the shore, when I noticed it. Floating."

Dale wrote, furiously, on his pad. "Go on."

"At first, I think animal—maybe deer. I've seen before. They sometime come to the river to die. So I steer in, get a better look. The wake from my boat, it cause the body to flip." He put his hand out, palm down, then quick-raised it to the ceiling. "That's when the smell hit me, and I get this awful feeling, right here." He closed his fist, punched himself on the breastbone, hard enough to hurt. "I knew right away it was her."

"Her?"

"The missing woman."

"I'm sorry," Dale said. "Je-... which missing woman?"

"The one with the eyes like Furini's Magdalene."

"Could you—do you know her name?"

"Laurie," he said. "Jessica Lynn." He flicked his hand at the wineglasses, hanging upside down overhead. "The one, they found her car in the parking lot."

Dale forced himself to breathe, evenly. *In. Out. In.* Every aspect of his bearing had to convey the polar opposite of surprise.

"I hate to have to ask this," Dale said. "I can imagine this must have been very hard on you, Mr. Moretti. But the body—it was in decent shape? You recognized her?"

He puffed out his cheeks, touched ten fingers above his drink, then drew them apart, slowly. "Bloated," he said. "Bad. But I recognize."

"How?"

"How does a salmon recognize her stream?"

"Right," Dale said. "But I mean, was there something specific? It might not have been her."

"I recognize her *face*," he said. "From the pictures!" He sliced his hand through the air again, nearly chopping Dale in the forehead. Dale followed his finger. There, on the wall next to the doorway, beneath a Last Voyage Saloon wall plaque, was the original "Missing" poster, with the photograph, circulated by Willamette PD.

"Got it," he said. "I'm sorry, Mr. Moretti. I just have to be sure."

Moretti let out a laugh. "Sure," he said, swirling his tumbler. "What's sure?"

"I suppose you're right about that."

"Reporter, I got a friend. From the club. We sit at this bar talking about it. He think Jessica was up to no good. Maybe selling drug, in the parking lot. My wife, she say the lady should never go out walking alone in the wood before dark. *Pazza!* she say. Tempting the fates. Know what I say?"

"What's that?"

"In my village, we have expression. 'After the ship has sunk, everyone know how she might have been saved.'"

"Mr. Moretti," Dale said. "Where do you live—currently?"

"Boxwood."

"And how old are you?"

"Sixty-eight. Sixty-nine in July."

"Would you mind if I took your picture? For the paper?"

Dale'd been saving this question for last. It wasn't something you put out there until you already had what you needed.

Moretti thought for a moment, shrugged. "It's okay."

He swiveled on the stool, crossed his arms, stern-faced. Dale pulled his camera from the bag, fired up the flash battery, waited for the high whine to dissipate. The two men eating in the dining room glanced over. Dale snapped a shot with a blinding flash. Then took a second—Moretti, a stone statue—and a third.

"One last thing?" he said. "Would you mind standing over there for me?"

Moretti glanced across the room. Pressed his lips together, understanding. Slid off the stool, sending it spinning. Shuffled along the bar and stood in the doorway. He crossed his arms and a vein in his neck bulged and crimped, and Dale released the shutter, framing the two of them, together.

As soon as Dale stepped into the hallway, the smell of newsprint and ink and Coffee-mate and stale Ginardi's pizza from 33,000 late night print runs hit him in the guts, as if it were a physical thing—as if it had mass and texture and responded to the laws of gravity, like a football, and he took a deep, centering breath. He passed the portrait of John Derrick, perched on a stool holding a cigarette—even the portraitist hadn't sought to hide the yellow cast of his subject's teeth or the cranky pitch of his brow. Dale picked up his pace as he moved along the Wall of Fame: plaque after plaque from the New Jersey Newspaper Association, honoring the *Herald* for excellence in feature writing and editing and layout and design, names of editors, reporters, and photographers carved into shimmering red plates, glued to faux mahogany. Dale didn't even look up when he passed the award he'd been a part of, Excellence in Breaking News, Second Place, for team coverage of the Danville pipeline explosion.

At the end of the hall, he pushed through the door, burst into the newsroom.

The sound changed, seamlessly. A half dozen reporters sat at desks in a long central island of cubicles, tapping keyboards, speaking in low voices, prying, manipulating, easing final tidbits of information from sources with laughter, empathy, or indignation. A television mounted to the wall above the Slot flashed muted images of a house fire on CNN. Gertie Parks scribbled something in blue on the assignment board, erasing something else with her elbow. Across the newsroom, roughly a fisherman's cast away, Simmons sat in his glass-walled office, arguing with the phone, phone cord coiled around his forearm like a ruby-red boa constrictor. "Yesterday!" he said.

If a voice could crack a walnut.

He slid past the first few cubicles to his desk, put his bag on his chair. He could see Rex Firestone's Kennedy-esque head of hair two cubicles up, and, in the adjacent workspace, V-Ray, tipped back, pen in her mouth, feet on her desk. He'd taken Firestone to Sal's just a few days before Missing Mom broke; V-Ray, in the summer of '87.

"Bowman!" Dale said.

He turned, a few steps from the darkroom, and Dale underhand-tossed his canister of film.

"Do me a favor and develop these. I need them for final."

It'd been a long time since he had this feeling: that every single person in the newsroom was aware of *him*. Waiting to see what *he* came up with.

"Dale."

He turned. "Hey, Cass."

"Mike wants you."

"Be in in a minute."

"He said: 'Immediately.'"

"Got it."

"He said to tell you: 'Immediately means immediately.' He said some other things, too."

"I'm sure," Dale said. "Tell him two seconds."

"One, two."

Dale rolled his eyes, brushed past her, stopping at the door with the engraved placard: *Managing Editor*.

Simmons sat at his desk, fingers flaying his keyboard, neck bent awkwardly, clamping the phone receiver to his shoulder, looking to all humanity as if he were trying to cut off either his own circulation or the phone's. His sleeves were in bunched cuffs above his elbows, revealing flaky whorls of psoriasis covering both forearms. A cigarette perched, incinerating, at the lip of a smokeless ashtray, but a thin film of smoke dulled every last surface anyway, from the golden heart-framed photograph of his wife and daughter to the Webster's New World hardcover that somehow always opened, when he dropped it on the floor to get someone's attention — a parlor trick he never tired of — to the page with the word *persevere*. Dale knocked on the window, and, as was his habit, he didn't wait for Mike to respond. He followed his knock right in.

"Uh huh," Simmons said. "Right." He shifted the phone to his white ear. "Hey listen, I gotta go." He hung up, looked at Dale. "Jesus, Tapper, I'm sitting here on goddamned pins and needles. What'dya stop for fucking coffee on the way in?"

"It's Missing Mom, Mike."

He let out a clipped breath. "Okay," he said. "Sit down."

"I found the guy that found her." Dale sat, pulled himself to the edge of the desk. "A fisherman. I just spent twenty minutes with him at the Esquand River Boat House. He's sure of it. I got it on the record."

"You've got that from the cops?"

"There's a 'Missing' photo up in the boat house, with her picture. He sees it every day. He recognized her face."

Simmons took off his glasses, rubbed his eyes with the meaty part of his palms, let out a slow breath. "You gave it a shot, Tapper."

"What do you mean, Mike? It's Laurie."

"Tapper, how long have you worked at this newspaper?"

"A long time."

"Long time, right. And in that time, have we ever run a story like this on one source? Without official confirmation?"

"This is all one big coincidence? A Jane in the river three days after a mom disappears? A fisherman who swears on the Holy Roman Empire it's her?"

"It *could* be a coincidence, Dale. That's the point. Now, give me six inches. 'Body found in Esquand. Police not releasing ID.' Then go home and get some rest. You look like crap."

Dale sighed, leaning back in his seat, gripping the armrests. "Give me five more minutes," he said.

"I don't have it," Simmons reached out for his phone, and Dale surprised himself: He slammed his hand on top of Simmons's on the receiver.

"Aren't we supposed to be the local 'paper of record'?"

"Get your hand off my hand, Dale."

"Three hundred seconds, Mike. That's all I'm asking for. Time it takes to make a Pop Tart."

"Tapper." He ripped his hand from under Dale's, slashing the receiver away. "This isn't a goddamned game. I've got a three-county newspaper that hits the streets in six hours. I want six inches. Make that four — 'Body found. No comment on Laurie' — then go the hell home."

Dale sprang up, as if someone'd sent an electric charge through his seat. He grabbed the dictionary, raised it high above the desk, dropped it squarely over Simmons's blotter. It hit with a loud, echoing *smack*. Dale was dimly aware of a rush of footsteps, behind him in the newsroom.

"How long have I worked at this newspaper?"

"Oh, for god's sakes."

"Twenty-one years, right. This is a big story. The biggest. All I'm asking is for is one more chance." He looked down at the open dictionary on the desk. He'd gotten lucky. "Remember?" Dale pointed to the page.

Simmons saw it, looked up at him, mouth closed. Then he shook his head slowly back and forth. "I shouldn't be doing this. Cassie's in a goddamned vice. You have five minutes, Tapper. Use it well."

Dale whirled and walked out, parting a cluster of staff that had assembled at the window.

"I thought you *shot* him," Cassie said.

"I thought he shot *you*," Gertie quipped.

Dale passed them, silently, in full stride. Moved his bag, dropped down on his chair. Dialed a number he knew by heart. It rang. It rang for fifteen seconds. Then fifteen more. "Answer the phone," Dale said.

"Dye, here."

Dale let out a breath. It was his first real break of the day.

Sgt. Dye was the evening shift commander. *Sergeant Dinosaur*, to the guys in the Slot. He was an old-timer, no doubt. Pushing mandatory retirement. But because he was an old-timer, he was also smart enough to understand that those articles about Lieutenant MacLachy—that was just a reporter doing his job. Ultimately, it was articles like those that gave police their legitimacy. If no one was keeping tabs on the cops, they'd abuse their power, and even if they didn't, people would assume they did. Over time, they'd lose the public trust and wouldn't be able to conduct so much as a routine traffic stop without handcuffs and billy clubs.

"Sarge," he said. "It's me."

"Hey, Scoop."

"I need your help."

"Glad to if I can."

"We have sources telling us on the record that Jessica Lynn Laurie's body turned up tonight. In the Esquand. Your jurisdiction."

Dale recognized the hard sucking sound Dye made with his teeth. "I can't comment on that, Scoop."

"Why not?"

"Everything goes through Chief tonight."

Dale grimaced. "Is Chief there?"

"Unfortunately, no."

"Sarge, our readership's on tenterhooks over this. If there's new information on the Laurie case, they have every right to know."

"There's nothing I can do, Scoop."

Dale huffed out a sigh, pushed up off his elbows. Felt himself deflating, heaviest bones sagging in. He looked up at the clock over the assignment board. Minute, minute and a half to go.

"Look, Sarge, we have all we need: The body found by a fisherman in the river today is none other than Jessica Lynn Laurie, of Willamette, New Jersey. Mother of two girls. Wife. Beloved daughter of the community. I just need to know if we're right."

"I told you, Dale. I can't say *anything*."

"I don't need you to *say* anything," Dale said, voice rising.

"You're losing me."

Dale glanced up at the clock.

"I'm going to count to ten. If we're wrong—hang up before I finish."

"Dale . . ."

Was there some faint hint of softening in his voice? Some trace easing up: the river, just after it wheels around the bend they call Round House Right.

"Sarge."

"My name is nowhere near this."

"On my honor."

"You said 'Hang up.'"

"Right."

And then Sgt. Dye said: "Start counting."

"One," Dale said, without pausing. "Two . . ."

Two cubicles up to the right, Firestone lifted his head above the prefab wall, put his arms out, elbows bent along the ridge, and perched, watching.

"Three . . . four . . . five."

V-Ray put her pen down, moved her feet off her desk, swiveled around in her chair, and leaned in with her chin on her fists. Chrissy Furlow stopped editing, angling her head so she could see Dale beyond her monitor.

"Six . . . seven . . . eight . . ." Dale said.

And Croyle was there, standing next to Dale's desk, hands on his hips, tongue tenting out his cheek.

"Nine . . ."

The first nine pins of that last frame, they fell like a flock of geese, Frank Carnevale had said. *I hit the headpin straight on, a perfect break. But that tenth . . . Well, I'm eighty-four-years young. I've been around a long time. But that was far and away the longest moment of my life. That pin wobbled and swayed, started down, swung right back up on a pencil point. I swear to God, I thought someone above the pit was holding it up with a wire. And then, I don't know what. Atlas shrugged, I guess.*

"Ten."

The empty sound in the phone was flawless. Dye was gone. Dale pressed the receiver to his ear. "Sarge?"

Had he heard something? Barely a sound at all.

"Okay, Dale," he said. "You didn't hear it from me."

PATAWAH VILLAGE—Authorities pulled the bloated body of Jessica Lynn Laurie, 33, from a shallow stretch of the Esquand River yesterday, seventy-two hours after her car was found in a small roadside parking lot off Route 19 in Willamette, the Herald Times has learned.

The body was discovered yesterday afternoon, officials confirmed, by an angler, fishing from his boat south of the Landing Lane Bridge.

"I had just cast near some reeds by the shore when I noticed it floating," the fisherman, Viggo Moretti, 68, of the Boxwood section of Willamette, told the Herald Times. "At first, I thought it was an animal—maybe a deer. I've seen them before. They sometimes come to the river to die. So I steered in to get a better look."

Moretti said the wake from his boat caused the body to flip over in the water and he saw her face. The body was bloated, he said, but recognizable.

"I knew right away it was her."

Authorities did not release any information about the cause of death. The body was scheduled to be transported to the Klamasink County Medical Examiner for an autopsy.

Laurie was last seen Monday night leaving Two Left Feet, the shoe store where she worked as an assistant manager.

The mother of 10- and 4-year-old girls and wife of a local bike mechanic inspired an outpouring of public sentiment in the days following her disappearance. Hundreds of volunteers combed the woods off Route 19, searching for clues. Classmates of the Lauries' daughters went door-to-door circulating missing posters, encouraging people to call a special tip line set up by the Willamette Police Department.

Her husband, Kevin, has said Laurie often hiked the Esquand River State Park trail, which begins at the parking lot where her car was discovered and connects to the towpath. Police said they found physical evidence placing Laurie both on the trail and at the river, near the abandoned Quality Cement Co. building.

Police, meanwhile, continue searching for a man they believe may have encountered Laurie on the trail the evening she *disappeared. They have circulated a composite sketch, calling him a "person of substantial interest" in the case.*

When he finished, he typed a final line: *Attempts to reach Jessica's husband Kevin for comment late last night were unsuccessful.*

Then he dialed the phone number Croyle had given him.

He knew no one would answer, and no one did.

"Please, watch your step," Jessica told him.

He pressed Enter. Sent the story to Simmons.

Dale opened his eyes. He'd woken at 7:05 — twenty-five minutes before his norm — unsure whether he'd dreamed it or the phone had actually been ringing. His heart raced. Pulitzer seemed to sense it. She twice jumped on the mattress, padded up the midline of his comforter, presented her star face to Dale, meowed, then purred. Meow. *Purr.* She nudged her nose into his armpit. Dale?

He threw off his comforter, sent Pulitzer skittering to the floor. In his bathroom, he brushed his teeth, stepped out of his briefs. Countless times in the shower he thought he heard the phone ring, but when he finally shut the faucets, the apartment was stone cold silent. He toweled dry, cleaned the wax out his ears with a Q-tip, stepped into trousers he'd left on the floor the night before. Then walked into the living room, buttoning his shirt. On the counter in the galley kitchen, the light on his answering machine was solid red. *Okay*, Dale thought. Five days since he'd filed his story, and he still hadn't been fired. "Alive and kicking," he said, out loud into the empty apartment. He flicked on his coffee machine, waited as it burbled and perked.

And then, standing in the entryway, he saw it — on the end table, next to the living room couch. The phone receiver, raised, ever-so-slightly on one end.

He stood for a moment, stock-still, head tilted — *was it really raised?* He walked to his door, opened it, picked up the *Herald*, then retreated to the kitchen, poured himself a cup of coffee, and made for his deck, glancing back once at the phone. *It was*, he thought. *Definitely. Off the hook.*

The sun was just peaking over the trees of the park, sending out wide rays of light. Dale slipped off the rubber band, opened the paper, unfolded it, and settled back on his plastic deck chair, ignoring the dew. Above the fold, a huge Bowman photo of Jessica Lynn Laurie smiling from her hospital bed, surrounded by Get Well balloons and flowers of every imaginable ilk, a daughter nestled under each armpit—the younger one with her eyes closed, her expression as close to pure bliss as might be captured on Kodachrome. It was a thing of beauty, really. Bowman had clicked the shutter at the exact right millisecond.

The 52-point headline ran the entire length of the page, starting over the text and finishing over the photo: 'My Daughters Kept Me Alive.'

Dale sipped his coffee. Planted his feet on the edge of a plastic table. Watched a flock of sparrows move over the park, drop toward the trees, then fling themselves back up at the clouds.

The article, written by Croyle, was based on an exclusive hospital bed interview he'd been granted by the family. Jessica trusted him. You could see that in *her* face, too. She wasn't about to hold back. A photo that would one day win a prize.

She had gone for a walk. She'd started at the parking lot and followed the trail, emerging a half hour or so later at the river. She'd lain on the planks of the dock, closed her eyes, felt the diminishing sun on her cheeks. And fallen asleep. Not long. But long enough that when she woke, there was barely any light left in the sky.

She started jogging up the towpath, found the trail, and headed back into the forest. Right away, though, she had a weird feeling—something was off. It'd been awhile since she'd been out there, but, still, she expected the trail to feel more familiar, somehow. It wasn't as well maintained as she remembered. Weeds and grass encroached from the edges. She had to walk over logs covered with thick, green moss. Wouldn't park rangers have cleared those by now? Also, it was surprisingly dark. She had no flashlight—no supplies at all—and already, the colors in the forest were starting to fade.

She picked up her pace, racing the sun. *This is right*, she thought. And, sure enough, rounding the base of a hill, the terrain seemed all at once recognizable. She thought she heard a car up ahead, and her heart beat hard with a vision of Route 19. She ran—ignoring the fact that the path she was following was hardly a path at all. Just a slightly better line between trees. She stopped, cocked her ear to the fast-coming night. Heard the creaking sway of a tree limb and high, rattling leaves. Felt the cold *surge, surge, surge* of her heart. *I have to retrace my steps,* she thought. *I have no choice.* Only, when she turned around—when she looked back—there was nothing there. No trail. No discernable path. It was as if she'd been lowered onto this spot from the stars.

She thought about the hikes her parents had taken her on when she was a girl, in and around Lake George. If you're ever lost in the forest, her dad had said. Stay put. You keep moving, you make a bad situation worse. *Okay,* she thought, her breath shallow. *I'm okay. It's chilly, but it's summertime. I can stay here tonight, and tomorrow, they'll find me.* She came upon a semiprotected spot in the hill she'd been traversing, an eroded cavern under some tree roots, and she lay down on the dirt, sheltered from the breeze. At some point, late that night, it started to rain, and she thought of her girls, and Kevin, and how maybe she wouldn't see them again, and she shook and shook and shook. She slept on and off, trembling, in one- or two-minute clips.

She survived drinking rainwater and eating wild blueberries and—when she realized she was really in trouble, when she thought she might be walking in circles, when she remembered from the sign at the trailhead that the park was roughly eighteen square miles—field crickets and pill bugs. It was her daughters, though. That's what gave her the strength to keep going. She was saved, in the end, by high tension wires. She'd climbed the highest tree she could find, spotted the wires way in the distance, and made for them—periodically climbing another tree, ignoring the raw scrapes on her forearms, and, if necessary, adjusting course. After another half day walking, she stumbled into a clearing at the base of a tower. Followed the wires—right out of the preserve.

Dale put the paper down and looked out over the twisted iron railing across the pea-green treetops of the park and the horizon blurred with his shame, and, at the same time, he'd never felt more gratitude for a person, ever. Not even remotely.

Because he'd be done. Surely, his career would be in ruins. But for one thing. Simmons had killed his story. Over Dale's strong objection, he'd killed it. *The confirm or hang up method is not an acceptable way to source a story,* he'd said. *Not in this newsroom. Not on a story this big.* Sitting in Simmons's office, the managing editor had in the end deflected Dale's last argument with a simple raised hand. Then, just as Dale's anger and frustration peaked, Simmons said he wanted Dale to take some time off. A full week, if not more. Paid, of course. Dale'd protested. But Simmons had closed the dictionary and pointed Dale out of his office. *You're not a spring chicken anymore, Dale,* he'd said. *Get some rest. And ease up on the coffee for a while, would you?*

Jessica had walked out of the forest two days later, bug-bitten, limping on a sprained ankle, past the point of exhaustion, but otherwise A-OK.

Dale glanced through the rest of the paper—noticed the short, unbylined brief in the blotter explaining that police had yet to identify a body found Thursday in the Esquand. Efforts were hampered by the fact that the body was badly decomposed and had likely been in the water for some time. They were culling through missing persons reports. It might be a vagrant, officials said, which could make it even more difficult to establish a positive ID. There was a chance, Dale knew, that they'd never ID the body. Sometimes, a Jane Doe stayed that way.

Dale went inside through the sliding patio door, looked again at the phone. Then, impulsively, he grabbed it. Put it to his ear. Heard nothing. No dial tone. Dead air. He thumbed the button on the cradle, held it down. When he released the button, the dial tone wailed in his ear. He looked at Pulitzer, looking at him. *How long had it been off the hook?* He dialed.

"Yeah!"

"Hey, Mike."

"Dale," he said. "I've been trying to call. You're line's been busy. You okay?"

"I'm fine," he said. "Resting, like you said to."

"That's good, Dale. Take the rest of the week. You need it."

"Mike," he said, "you still want me to come back?"

"As opposed to?"

"That was a pretty big gaffe I made."

"Almost made."

"A little too close for comfort, don't you think?"

"Don't flatter yourself, Dale. It wasn't that close."

He thought about the news staff, gathered at the door of Mike's office. Saw Croyle, standing at his desk with his cheek tented out. Pictured himself leaving Simmons's office, walking with his head down between the cubicles. "I was thinking about calling it quits, to be honest," he said.

Mike laughed. "To do what?"

"I don't know. Haven't figured that out yet. Something else."

"Dale, you couldn't shine a shoe."

"Thanks for making me feel better."

"They don't pay me to make my reporters feel better." Dale heard the draw of a cigarette through pinched lips. The exhalation of smoke. "Take care of yourself, Dale. I'll see you Monday."

Dale could still picture Woodward, sitting on the edge of the news editor's desk, legs dangling over the side. High cheekbones; dark hair raked to his right; dimpled, almost girlish smile. Tie loose at his neck, as if he'd come straight from the office after a hard day's work taking down the President of the United States.

It was just a few years post-Watergate. Woodward, an old friend of Abe Kesting's from Yale, had taken care of his business on the story — spent twenty or so minutes on the phone with his editors in Washington — and, now, to return the favor before heading back to D.C, he was shooting the shit with half a dozen staffers.

"So, Bob," Kesting said, at some point, "tell us: What's the most important lesson you learned on the story?"

"You know," Woodward began, leaning in, "there was a moment, when we were covering the trial — before everything broke wide open. The prosecutor was painting the whole thing as a low-level conspiracy. A couple operatives had been paid a few grand to gather intelligence on their political enemies. No more, no less. Case closed.

"Carl and I might have taken our foot off the pedal right there, except it didn't make sense. Why would they go through all the trouble of breaking into Democratic headquarters? Why would the Committee to Re-elect the President take such a huge risk for two-bit intelligence readily available from local police?

"When I was in college," he continued, "an instructor assigned us to read some medieval documents with conflicting accounts of King Henry the Fourth's famous walk to Canossa in 1077. The king had angered Pope Gregory—he'd been excommunicated—and had crossed the Alps seeking forgiveness. We were supposed to write a report, outlining what happened. I was up all night, poring over documents, taking notes. I based my write-up on the central, undisputed fact upon which all witnesses agreed: the king had waited in the snow for days, hoping to regain the Pope's favor. Barefoot.

"Well, I was pretty proud of my shiny penny of a paper. But guess what? My professor failed me. And I deserved it. Because the fact is, *no one* could stand barefoot in the snow that long. Their feet would freeze. They'd die of hypothermia. As our teacher told us: 'The divine right of kings does not extend to overturning the laws of nature—and common sense.'"

Was it a trick of memory, or had Bob Woodward looked right at Dale when he said: "No matter what anyone tells you, no matter how compelling something seems, always, always use common sense"?

Dale had written an article once on the Esquand River—its industrial history, the battle against pollution, modern day emergence as a recreational hub. The headline had come from a poem, struck like spark from flint one night by an eighteenth-century bargeman, heading passively toward the sea: *Thou Queen of Rivers, Esquand.* Few people he met knew it, but the river's name came from an Indian word meaning "door" or "entrance," to the Atlantic. That is, it flowed *east.* Patawah Village, where the body had been found, was *west* of the clearing where they'd discovered the physical evidence. If a body had gone into the water off the pier at the abandoned concrete plant, it couldn't surface in Patawah. The river runs in the opposite direction.

And Dye. Dye was a senior citizen. Out of the loop, though he liked to think he was in it. He thought the *Herald* already had the story on the record. He might have been confirming the same rumor Hawker'd heard over the scanner. A perfect circle of innuendo. As for Moretti—well, Moretti was in love, and a little drunk. He would have seen Jessica's face in the clouds, or the patchwork limbs of the magnolia trees, or the swirling graffiti on the concrete abutment of the bridge. He himself had told Dale the body was badly bloated—it had clearly been in the water a while. Moreover, if there had been even the slightest chance that it was Missing Mom's body in the river—well, their competitors all had sources, too. Wouldn't there have been other reporters? Even one? Simmons had seen that, right away. Why hadn't *he*?

That was the worst part. Dale couldn't say. He couldn't say where he'd gone astray, why his instincts had misled him, or how he might do things differently next time. Sure, looking back, there were red flags aplenty. But sometimes, in a moment, you're carried along by something that isn't nailed down—something propulsive and intense and irresistible—and you don't stop, you fail and fail and fail to check yourself, and then, all of a sudden, when you turn around and look back, there's nothing there.

There was the building. One story, 150-feet long, orange brick, and windowless on this side, save for a single square pane on the back door, and a small bank at the far corner, where visitors parked for reception. There was the flag, ten-foot-tall Goudy Old Style letters marching across the flat roof, visible from the highway, abandoned, thick-stick hawk's nest in the crook of the lowercase "r." There, by the steps, was the patch of grass where Perkins and Furlow and sometimes Van Dorn went to smoke and pace.

He didn't have to go in. He didn't have to look Croyle in the eye or face Rex Firestone's earnest disappointment. He could just get back in his car and drive. Who'd ever miss him?

As soon as Dale stepped into the hallway, the smell of news-print and ink and Coffee-mate and stale Ginardi's from 33,000 late night print runs hit him in the guts, as if it were a physical thing, like a football. He took a deep, centering breath, and headed for the newsroom.

Mainlanders

We rode our bikes through a gateway, between two old whale lookouts linked by a twenty-foot-long banner— "Welcome to Summer"—a trident-wielding mariner standing sentinel over the final "r." A few island moms were fussing over deep tin dishes, removing foil from littlenecks, adjusting burners under weakfish stew and Jersey corn chowder. A double-decker barbecue belched saffron-shrimp smoke. Girls jumped double Dutch in the side lot, and high school kids played basketball against the old Coast Guard building at a hoop with a metal chain net.

"Do you see them?" I said, standing on my pedals.

Tubby shook his head.

"What if they don't show?"

"They'll show."

I spit my gum into a garbage barrel. "We should've done it yesterday, when we had the chance."

"Swanny," he said, "if a fluke were right-eyed, it'd be a flounder."

I snorted, coasting. It was just one of those things people said in Bay City, and when they said it, you knew exactly what they meant.

We'd first spotted the girls on Memorial Day, six days before, lying facedown on matching towels at the Sixth Street Beach, bikini tops unsnapped. Walked by on our way to the water, close as we could without kicking sand in their hair. We bodysurfed awhile, sneaking glances up the beach between rides, always aware of where they were. When the tide drew us south, we churned our way north until we'd drawn even again. They were about our age. And the whole time we were in the water, we never saw any boyfriend types approach.

Thereafter, we were on the Sixth Street Beach every day. We sucked in our stomachs, puffed up our chests, selected the biggest waves and rode them all the way into the sand crab zone, a skipped shell from their sun-kissed toes. And if they happened to look up or god forbid smile—if they made even fleeting eye contact—our entire world opened up, and every other thing in our lives, good, bad, or ugly, sloughed away.

On the fifth day, we screwed up our courage and followed them home, a couple of James Bonds, dodging for cover every time they turned, crouching behind parked cars. At one point, we cut between houses and, without meaning to, came out on the road in front of them just as they approached, yakking up a storm, beach chairs and bags slung over their shoulders. For three blissful, godforsaken, can't-ever-get-them-back seconds, maybe four, we'd stood, facing them. My mouth opened and closed without a sound, seagull-like. Mercifully, they never looked up. They walked right by.

That's when we swore to each other: if they showed up at Mariner Fest, we'd make our move. Come hell or high water.

We lived on a barrier island, eighteen miles long, a mile at sea, thin as a pipefish, that slashed up the New Jersey coast on a diagonal. Once upon a time, there'd been a ferry service from Shady Cove and train lines from Philly and New York, but when we were kids, the only way on or off without a boat was via the Causeway—four lanes, two in each direction—a bridge with tubular fluorescent rails that skipped across the Great Bay in two arches, major and minor, like a rainbow with a little extra gas. Back then, before Hurricane Gloria took it down, arriving tourists were greeted with a wooden sign: "Welcome to Bay City Island, Home to 5,118 of the Friendliest People on the Jersey Shore, Plus a Couple of Soreheads."

Up 'til then, we'd gone to school on the island our whole lives, kindergarten through eighth grade, with the same twelve kids in our class, give or take, and the girls—Cathy, Amy, Jessica, Julia, Penny, Cassidy, and Lauralie—we'd known since we were embryos. That neither Tubby nor I had ever had a girlfriend wasn't for lack of masturbating. It seemed as if we'd loved them all, at one time or another. But I was the "nice" kid—Lauralie trusted me enough to tell me all about the high school junior she was going with; Penny, to let me carry her books between classes—and Tubby was the "funny" one, famous for the time he put the whoopee cushion under the librarian's seat just before she sat down, otherwise known as "The Fart Heard 'Round the World." We envied Dredge Stiles, who was going with Michelle Willow, a seventh-grader whose quiet shyness only made her that much more desirable. Michelle, who had innocently brushed her chest ever-so-barely against my arm in the lunch line once, emptying my mind of all other thoughts for a week. How to get from "nice" and "funny" to Michelle Willow—what it would be like to kiss a girl and have her kiss you back—these were among the universe's most perplexing and distracting questions.

With these girls, though, we sensed opportunity. A change in the weather so to speak. They were Mainlanders. They didn't know us from Neptune. It was a chance for Tubby and me to be Tubby and me, free and easy. If we could just find a way to say "hi"—if we could somehow take a step over the terrifying, stupefying fault line that separated the have-nots from the haves—we figured we had pretty decent odds.

I'd all but given up hope. We'd been there half an hour, circled the lot three times. Laid our bikes in the sand and split up, weaving through a cast of thousands, coming back together at the buffet. We'd taken turns standing on Shelia DuPree's step stool. I was fairly well convinced they weren't coming. Maybe they hadn't seen the flyers on the telephone poles or bait shop bulletin board. That's when I noticed Tubby, standing next to the barbecue, hands on hips, staring across the lot — utterly oblivious to the fact that the breeze had shifted, redirecting the smoke, surrounding him in a blue-gray charcoal haze.

"Thar she blows," he said.

I turned quickly, following his gaze, and felt a shark-in-the-water shot of nerves: the girls were heading right for us.

The one I'd been eyeing all week held a big plastic bowl to her chest. She wore a maroon T-shirt — USC-something — and cutoff blue jeans, frayed at the edges. The other was decked out in a red and white striped shirt and white shorts that showed off her tan. She held a small teal purse at her hip.

"Showtime," Tubby said.

"They're here."

"And you're on."

"I'm not sure I can do this."

"You can. Trust me."

"Maybe you should go first."

"Swanny. We drew punks."

I let out a hard breath. They stopped, scanned the lot. Miss USC pointed and her friend peeled off on a rope for the port-o-john. Then, without further delay, she kept right on coming.

"Best two out of three."

He lowered his voice. "This is our last chance, Swanny!"

"I know," I whispered. "But Tub. Seriously. She's so effin' *hot*."

That's when he shoved me. And when Tubby Boyd shoved you, it was no small thing. I nearly fell right into her, just as she was on final approach. Somehow, I managed to right myself, pulling up behind her. She must have felt my breeze, though, because she turned and smiled. Looked right at me, in fact, with light brown eyes that shined like treasure in a chest. And the only thing I could remember were the pickup lines Tubby's older brother Ray had given us. He said they were surefire winners at the clubs.

Are those space pants you're wearing? Cause your ass is out of this world.

She lowered her eyes, leaned over, placed her bowl of fruit salad on the buffet.

All those curves, and me with no brakes.

Removed the Saran, balled it, stepped back from the table. A second more, and she'd be gone.

"Is there an airport nearby, or is that just my heart taking off?"

She half turned and looked at me. A smattering of freckles, winter-flounder brown, spread across her nose and under her eyes. I gripped my lifelines, hard as I could. *Apologize,* I thought. *Blame Ray. Blame Tourette's. Blame it on Rio.*

"Do you have any overdue library books?"

I looked at her, brow furrowed. "Do I . . . ?"

"Have any overdue library books," she repeated.

"I . . . we don't . . . library books? Why?"

"Cuz you've got the word 'fine' written all over."

She smiled. I felt myself sway, ever-so-slightly, like the lighthouse in a small craft advisory.

"We've seen you guys at the beach," she said, nodding at Tubby behind me.

"You have?"

"Wasn't that you? Bodysurfing?"

"Might've been."

"It was," she said. "Nice form."

"Oh," I said. "Jeeze. Thanks."

She glanced down at her fruit salad. Again, I felt sure she was going to skedaddle. Leave me there with my mouth slung low and my heart pumping like a bilge on a sinking ship. She looked across the lot and put a hand over her eyes, a sun shield. When her friend emerged from the john, she waved and just started walking.

"You a Trojans fan?" I said.

She spun fast, eyes narrowed. *"Excuse me?"*

I pointed at her T-shirt—*USC Football*—tucked neatly into shorts that hugged her hips.

"Oh," she said. "USC. My uncle teaches there. He's a film-maker. James Earl Jones came to his class once."

"James Earl Jones?"

"Um, Darth Vader?"

"Oh!" I said. Then, imitating Vader's voice: "Remember the Force."

Remember the fucking force? What the hell was I thinking?

That's when she said: "I like a boy with a little Dark Side in him."

Once, on a sixth-grade field trip, we visited a fire zone in the Pine Barrens. On one side of the road was a regular forest. The other was burned to a crisp. We walked into the char a ways, smoke-stink rising up all around us, and then our teacher bent, picked up a pinecone. It was interstellar black. Something you'd find in five-alarm ruins. But when he turned it, we saw it had cracked open. A tiny green sapling sprouted from the center. Intense heat causes the pinecone to burst, he explained, so life can begin anew. Standing there, an arm's length from Miss USC, that's exactly how I felt.

Her hair was sun-streaked blonde, pulled back in a ponytail, her boobs, three clams out of ten on our rating scale, which, for me, was more than plenty. The wind pivoted, and, like a sudden gift, I could smell her—a brain-jamming swirl of some kind of wild beach blossoms. I sniffed silently, lips shut tight.

"Penn State," she said, after a moment. "My dad went there. The Nittany Lions—that's my favorite team."

For a split second, I thought to say something about my dad, but he hadn't gone to college. So I stuck out my hand.

"I'm Nick. Nick Swan."

She took it and shook. "Well, hello there, Mr. Nick," she said. "I'm Anna. And this"—she forked a thumb over her shoulder as her friend pulled up behind her—"is my best friend, Caitlyn."

"Hi, Caitlyn." I waved. She was shorter and roundish, with dark curly hair—Tubby'd dubbed it "mahogany," but it wasn't quite. Either way, her rack was impressive: a solid six clams.

Caitlyn pressed her lips together and nodded, then smiled. "Hey."

I guess he'd seen about all he could stand, because he was next to me in a flash. "And this is Tub—"

"*Thomas*," he said, overriding me. He reached out and confiscated Caitlyn's hand in his mitts. "Thomas Boyd. It's a pleasure. And, might I add—on behalf of my dad, Slouch Boyd, Mayor, and my mom, Veronica, president of the Bay City Neighborhood Association, Welcome to Bay City, New Jersey."

Anna's eyebrows arched. "Your father's *mayor*?"

"And *plumber*," Tubby said. "And *his* dad"—he whacked me on the back—"Captain of the Miss Bay City, fishing boat of the stars."

"Wow." Anna nodded, eyebrows raised. "What stars?"

"Well, not exactly 'stars,' per se."

Tubby's eyes widened, incredulous. "Ricky Schroeder's not a star?"

"Ricky Schroeder was on your dad's boat?"

"That's true," I said. "Ricky Schroeder. He caught an oyster cracker."

"Did you *touch* him?"

"Well, yeah. I took him off the hook. You can do it with pliers, if you're careful."

"Not the oyster-thingy!" Anna said, wrinkling her nose. "*Ricky*!"

"Oh, sure. Yeah. I must've. He gave me a twenty-dollar tip."

Anna clapped her hands five times fast, fingers pointing heavenward. "Did you hear that, Caitlyn?"

"Holy smokes."

"Which hand did he touch?"

"I guess, this one, I guess."

She reached and took it—snatched it right out of thin air. "I'll never wash my hand again."

"No," Tubby said. "I wouldn't."

She dropped my hand, and it swung to my side, fingers curled, one hundred percent Neanderthal.

"Speaking of which," Tubby said, "Nick and I were just about to wade over and get us some grub. How 'bout we fix you gals a couple of plates? We know what's good."

It was the greatest non sequitur in all of recorded time. Not bad for a guy who whacked off to bra ads in the Sears catalog.

We scrambled off to the buffet. "Swanny," he said, once we were out of their orbit. "We're *in*." I glanced over my shoulder. I half expected to see Drew Johnson sidling in to make his move. Or Dredge Stiles—girls were drawn to him like blues to chum. But Anna and Caitlyn were standing there, right where we'd left them, gabbing, animated, drawing stories in the air with their hands. Awaiting our return.

At the buffet, we cut in line—"Scuze me, pardon me, Welcome Committee, official business"—and made up plates for the girls and ourselves. We stuffed our pockets with napkins and Diet Cokes, then brought it all back and led them along the sandy edge of the lot to Belle's Bench, spit up by the bay during the hurricane in '76. Tubby motioned for the girls to sit, and they did, adjusting themselves, plates on laps. We sat at their feet, on the sand.

"So," Anna said, settling back, slipping out of her flip-flops, "you guys actually *live* here, huh?"

"Three hundred sixty-five days a year," Tubby said. "Sixty-six in a leap year."

Caitlyn smiled. "You're funny."

"Funny ha ha, or funny peculiar?"

"Funny—I don't know. Both?" She looked at Anna. "Am I allowed to say that?"

Anna shrugged, lifting the corner of her sea basserole with her fork, checking underneath. "What's it like? Living here?"

"Exactly like anywhere else," Tubby said. "Only, a million times better."

"It's cool," I said. "I can see the ocean from my window at school."

"Nick, by the way—you should know, Anna—he's the reigning Bay City Search and Rescue Champion, Junior Division."

"What's that?" She forked a bite of basserole, chewing carefully, mouth closed.

"It's no big deal," I said.

"It's a deal," Tubby said. "One of the biggest. Tell 'em Nick."

"It's a competition."

"You have to hold your breath, under water, for like a half an hour . . ."

"Two minutes, Tub. Don't get carried away."

". . . and rescue a drowning dummy in four-foot seas."

"A dummy?" Caitlyn said. "Why not someone smart?"

"*Ba dump bump!*" Tubby said, slapping out the beat on his thighs. "We got a live one, Nick! Oh, and then there's the dreaded fender race. Nick won it going away."

Anna swigged her Coke. "Fender race?"

"Try swimming through the surf to a marker and back—half mile each way—with a fender tied to your ankle on a four-foot rope."

I could see by Anna's face the explanation only went so far.

"A fender's like a buoy. It's inflatable. You put 'em between the hull of a boat and the pier when you're docking. Keeps the fiberglass from getting dinged up. When you're swimming, if you tie one to your ankle, it gives you a little extra drag in the water. It's not hard, if you practice."

"Not hard my ass."

"Sounds hard," Anna said.

"Might as well pull a dead cormorant through the water," Tubby said.

"So, if I were drowning in the high seas," Anna said, reaching out with her bare foot and knocking mine playfully to the side, "you'd save me?"

"Well . . . there'd be a lifeguard."

"He'd save you," Tubby said. "You can write that down."

"It doesn't really matter." Caitlyn wiped a spot of corn butter from her mouth. "We won't go in anymore, anyway."

Tubby's brow pinched. He put a hand over his heart, as if he were about to recite the pledge of allegiance. "*Excusaymwah?*"

"She's right," Anna said. "Too many jellyfish."

"Jellies never hurt anyone," I pierced a shrimp with a toothpick.

"They hurt me! I got stung!" Caitlyn piped, rotating her arm. There was a little redness and a patchy scab where she'd picked at it. "Nasty little squishy creatures. There's *zillions* of them."

"It's a problem," Anna agreed. "Your dad's mayor? Maybe he can do something about it?"

"About *jellies?*"

"I don't know—scoop 'em out? With a big net? It's really lame."

"Scoop 'em," Tubby repeated, as if the idea might actually have some merit, "with a net."

Anna nodded. "Do you have, like, a suggestion box or something?"

"A what now?"

"You know, where we could put cards? For improvements?"

"We don't," Tubby said. "You're the first to mention it, as far as I know."

"You might consider it," Caitlyn said. "It's fairly basic."

"It's not the worst idea. It's not rear-ending a Pinto. I bet Slouch'd consider it. As far as jellyfish go, though . . ."

"Jellyfish are *numero uno*. We have other suggestions, don't we, Cait?"

"Greenheads!"

"Ouch!" Anna said. "*Blood suckers*. Get rid of those."

"We do spray, I know that. There's only so much we can do."

"What about the humidity?" Caitlyn said. "Can you do something about that? My hair's a disaster zone."

Tubby separated his paper plates, pulling a clean one out from under one soaked with baked-bean juice. He asked for a pen. Caitlyn unzipped her purse, fished around, tossed one over. Across the top Tubby wrote: *Suggestions*. Then, beneath that, he started a list. "Jellyfish. Check. Greenheads. Check. Humidity. Check. Anything else?"

"Now that you asked," Anna said, looking over her knees at Tubby's plate. "Put down: 'More to do.'"

"Okay, hold the phone," I said. "This is *Bay City*, for god's sakes!"

Anna shrugged, lips pursed, two palms up. "Can we help it if we're bored?"

"You must be the first. Someone call Guinness Book."

On his plate, Tubby wrote: *More to do.*

"Have you been fishing?"

"I get seasick."

"Crabbing? You can drop a trap from any pier."

"Why would we want to catch *crabs*?"

"What about shell-skipping?"

"Oh, gee," Caitlyn said. "Hours and hours of entertainment!"

"It is if you keep score."

"Have you been to the Galleon? At Pier 18?" Tubby tried. "Home of Krinkle Fries—voted Tastiest Snack on the Island, four years running. Try 'em with the pickle juice fry sauce and your world will never be the same."

"Is that the one with the pirate?" Caitlyn wanted to know.

"You've been?"

"Blimey!" Anna said. "What's a pirate's favorite letter?"

She was imitating Captain Krinkle, who roved the food court galleon with a parrot on his shoulder, hustling patrons for laughs.

"Arrrrrrrrrr," Caitlyn answered, in her very best pirate-ese.

"What kind of socks does a pirate wear, matey?"

Caitlyn slashed an imaginary saber through the air. "Arrrrrrrrrgyle."

"That's good," Tubby said. "You guys should really consider taking your act on the road."

"We're not going back there," Caitlyn said, putting her plate down on the bench next to her. "That parrot is a health code violation waiting to happen."

That's when the conversation stopped, faster than a sailboat in irons. For a moment, we looked at each other. Me at Anna at Caitlyn at Tubby at me. It was as if a wormhole'd opened up and swallowed the English language, aardvark to zygote. Anna put her plate down. Placed her hands on the edge of the bench, waiting for whatever was going to happen next.

There was one more line. I'd gotten it from the Bazooka Joe comic, on our way over that afternoon. It never in a million years occurred to me I'd have to use it. But this was a break-the-glass, rip-the-fire-alarm moment. And I was all out of options.

"Anna," I said. "Do you have any raisins?"

She looked at me cross-eyed. "Raisins?"

"Yeah," I said. "Raisins? Do you have any?"

"Well, let's see, I don't know. Not that I'm aware. What about you, Cait? Any raisins on you by chance?"

"Not a single one to speak of," she said.

"Then how 'bout a date?"

Anna laughed.

I put my plate down. Stood. I could feel my pulse firing in my neck. All their eyes on me. "You want fun, meet us at the bay beach tomorrow, eight A.M. sharp."

"What for?"

"A surprise," I said. "A true blue Bay City experience."

Tubby looked at me, seeing where I was headed, slow grin rising.

"Tell us!" Anna said.

"Sorry. No can do."

"You *have* to!"

"If we told you," Tubby said, "we'd have to kill you."

"Hardy har hardly," Caitlyn said, through her nose.

"We can make you tell," Anna said, letting her smile inch up, reaching out, tucking a loose curl behind my ear.

For a moment, I forgot to breathe. I was 20,000 leagues under the sea without a scuba tank, the spot behind my ear reverberating.

"Yeah?" I managed. "How's that?"

"We have our ways."

"Forget it," Tubby said, coming to my rescue. "You wanna play, you gotta pay. Tomorrow. Eight A.M. Come see for yourselves."

She sighed, dramatically. "What do you think, Cait? A mystery date with Bay City's First Son and Search and Rescue Champ, Junior Division?"

"I hate surprises."

"Come on!" Anna said. "It'll be fun. Remember what your mom said? *Carpe diem, quam minimum credula postero!*"

"Yeah," Tubby said. "Or remember what my mom says: *Ipso facto, e pluribus unum con carne.*"

This time, they both laughed. "I think I'm in love," Caitlyn said.

Rarest of rarities, Tubby nearly blushed.

"So, you're in?"

"It's a date!" Anna stood, reaching for Caitlyn's hand, pulling her off the bench. "Nick, Thomas, we'll see you tomorrow! It was nice to meet you boys. We have to go report to our moms. We're all supposed to go the Pancake House!"

"Chow!" Caitlyn added, swiping her hand across the air as if defogging a bathroom mirror.

Anna smiled, Queen of the Prom, and then they ran back toward the crowd, hand-in-hand, leaving picked-over paper plates and soda cans on the bench behind them, looking back once, for good measure.

It'd happened sudden as a sandstorm, but we both felt it. It wasn't just Tubby and me anymore. It was Tubby and Caitlyn, and me and Anna, with the tropic-night smell of just lit tiki lamps on the air and eons to go before Labor Day in what was fast shaping up to be the summer of our lives.

Our bare feet broke through a crust of dark sand drenched by an overnight soaker, making soft prints in the dry sand underneath. We passed through a slat wood-and-wire fence, between low dunes, across an area with knee-high beach grass, taking care not to step on burrs. I carried the bucket, a dinged-up metal pail. Tubby held the net in the crook of his arm. We'd stayed out late the night before, telling anyone and everyone who would listen about our good fortune, and while we were bone-tired, we couldn't have cared less.

At the edge of the bay, I twisted the bucket into the sand. Then Tubby and I stood facing each other—he holding his post, me holding mine—and walked backwards, unrolling the net. With the brown mesh fully stretched out between us, eight feet apart, we shook—up together, down together, up together—releasing a cascade of sand, freeing a few strands of dried black seaweed from our previous trip.

The girls' voices came to us on a scrap of breeze just as we were about to get started, and when we turned to look, there they were, rounding the bulkhead.

"Right on time," Tubby said.

Just seeing Anna made me crazy all over.

She wore a white sundress, ruffled over her boobs, with a flower pattern—a dazzle of colors and kinds—to her knees, a single strap over her collarbone, tied in a ribbon behind her neck. Her hair was out of the ponytail, lying wavy over one shoulder, and her eyes seemed lighter somehow, as if they still had some dream left in them. As I watched, she half turned on the ball of her foot to wipe sand off her leg. The site of all that bare back almost knocked me flat.

"What's *that*?" Caitlyn said, pointing. She wore an electric pink dress, smooth on the bottom, crinkly on the top, with oversized matching shell earrings.

"Seining net," Tubby said. "We're gonna catch us some bait!"

"Our date's after?"

"This *is* the date," I said.

Anna tilted her head, looked at the net from an angle, as if it were some kind of curious deep sea relic. When she spoke, her voice had zero inflection: "You brought us here to watch you catch bait?"

"Not just any bait," Tubby said. "*Sand eels.* Specialty bait. You can't buy them in stores. And fluke can't resist 'em. They go gaga for 'em."

"My dad gives them out on his boat, Anna. Keeps the fishermen happy. Pretty much guarantees a catch."

"We'll probably land a doormat this afternoon," Tubby said. "You'll want to check the papers."

"Wow. We were guessing a picnic," Caitlyn said. "Some bagels and cream cheese, maybe. Fresh strawberries. Definitely didn't see this coming."

"Anyone can have a picnic. You guys are in for a treat. Not one other visitor on the island will ever see anything like this. Grab a seat and prepare to be utterly amazed."

Anna glanced up the beach. "Where are we supposed to sit?"

"Your towels?"

"We didn't bring *towels*," Caitlyn said.

The four of us stood there in an approximate diamond, with me and Anna the closer points. Considering the upshot.

"They can sit on the bulkhead," Tub said, looking at me.

"No, no, no. Oozing with tar. They'll ruin their snazzy outfits. Stay here a sec. Tub, follow me."

I ran up the shoreline, Tubby padding behind, to the top of a sculpted slope of sand—highest point on the bay beach, thanks to the steady seasonal wind funnel along the spit—and looked down. There, trapped in the hollow between dunes, were planks of driftwood, smoothed by the tides and warming in the sun.

Tubby nodded, tongue popping out between closed lips. In less than half a minute, we were back with the girls, wedging a five-foot plank into the beach, brushing off stubborn kernels of sand. "Girls," I said, slapping my hands together. "Bleacher seats."

"Thanks, MacGyver," Caitlyn said.

"Don't mention it!"

"Are you boys really going in?" Anna asked, smoothing her dress underneath her and taking a seat. "It's freezing!"

I licked my finger and stuck it in the air. "Nah!" I said. "Remember who you're talking to!"

Even though that's what I said, I had to admit she was right. It was a hazy morning, sun stuck low in the sky. One of those mornings you wished for a wet suit—and all we had were bathing suits and T-shirts. The rain had churned up the bay, leaving it a cloudy, briny smudge, and a chill had lodged in the sand, where it had no business being. The mussel bed was totally underwater, revealed only by the seaweed tips rippling the surface. The eels, if we were lucky, would be congregating in schools along the perimeter. It was the perfect time to hit.

We walked to the edge of the bay, leaving the girls at the crest. With the net spotless, Tubby and I angled our poles toward the water and waded in. One step, two steps, three steps, bracing for the chill. The brown mesh bloomed out behind us. We dunked our balls and resumed breathing.

Tubby had the inside position, working along the mussel bed. I held the outside, watching for telltale ripples, back slightly hunched—inside arm high, outside arm in the water, keeping the rod tip in the sand so the fish couldn't swim under the net. We walked steady, step-for-step. When we reached the first turn, I pivoted, water over my waist, and we rushed the outer ridge. We couldn't see the fish—the bay was way too murky—but we could feel them, a thousand and one mini vibrations in our posts.

"Big haul."

Tubby nodded, breathing hard, working his stick along the ridge, turning up a muddy wake. "Wait 'til they see this," he said. "They'll never leave."

We pulled the net forward and fell quiet. They would, of course—leave. At some point. Mainlanders always eventually did.

Tossing and turning in my bed the night before—with sleep increasingly impossible—I'd already started thinking about what it would take to visit them in their hometowns, wherever they might be. True, there was no precedent for it. And there was no public transportation off the island. But there was a bus depot on the other side of the Causeway. We could bike there and from there, catch a Coast City to pretty much anywhere. I'd checked the *Beachcomber* that morning. Fares started at $2.10 and ran to 30 bucks. It wouldn't necessarily be easy. But we'd find a way. We were thirty yards apart and a stiff breeze was blowing onshore and I could still smell Anna's hair. We all but had to.

We hit the far edge of the mussel bed. My arms strained against the weight of the net. Tubby slowed so I could pivot. We made a hard sweep to shore.

As we came out of the water, we turned up our posts, net sagging heavily between us. Walked up the beach and laid the net across the sand. Tubby charged the bucket. I waved the girls down.

"Jackpot!" I gestured with an open palm, allowing myself a smile. There must have been fifty good-sized sand eels slithering snake-like around the net. A small calico skittered sideways over a pipefish, dodging wads of seaweed, claws raised in warning. Killies flung themselves hither and yon, and sand shrimp snapped off the mesh, as if electrified. A tiny flounder did a backflip, landing white side up. There were mussels, clumped together, still gripping chunks of bed, and lodged in that sinewy dirt, I knew, was a potpourri of the smallest sea creatures you could see with the naked eye. It was a microcosm of everything, absolutely everything the bay had to offer, in one haul.

"Voilà!" Tubby said, returning with the bucket, breathing hard, sweating. He put it down, water sloshing up over the sides.

"Did we tell you, or did we tell you? You won't see this at the multiplex."

"Wow," Anna said. She was standing three steps back with her arms crossed. "Bait."

"*Sand eels,*" Tubby said, working over the net, dropping fistfuls of fish in the bucket.

I reached down and plucked one of the bigger ones. It was cold and smooth in my hand, maybe five inches long, white-bodied with a copper stripe running the length of his back. Black pupil, ringed yellow. I held my hand out to Anna and opened my fingers carefully so she could see, cupping my palm. The eel opened and closed its bony mouth a few times and then stopped, dead.

"Cute," Anna said.

Caitlyn flattened her face. "Ugh," she said. "They *stink*."

I looked at her, shifting my jaw starboard to port. Tossed the eel underhand into the bucket. Tubby caught the calico by its hind leg and side-armed it, sending it spinning out over the drink. A black-headed gull snared it, dipped his wing, and veered over our heads, gobbling the crab in midair.

"There's a fair chance I'm about to be sick," Anna said.

"I already am."

"You know what?" Anna said. "It's getting late. We should go. We have to meet our moms."

Caitlyn touched her nose and pointed at Anna.

"Wait . . . what?"

"At the Pancake House. They'll be wondering where we are."

"But—you told them you're on a date! With us."

"How do you know what we told them?"

"You can't go yet!" I said. "We're just getting started."

"We get the idea, Nick," she said. "Sand eels! *Yay!*" She made two tight fists and shook them, as if holding pompoms. "You guys are really onto something here. Keep up the good work. Come on, Cait, let's go."

I looked at Tubby, whose hound-dog eyes said it was all up to me, all over again. I had to do something, fast.

I caught her in a few loping steps. "Listen, Anna, what if we take you guys to Kramer's tonight? They just opened. It's a total scene. The amusement park. They've got a giant Ferris wheel. Best view of the island, hands down. You'll love it."

"As much as this?" She reached out, lifted my face with a finger, fluttering my heart. "Maybe another time, Nick."

"Well, just hang on two secs. Let us walk you to the Pancake House and plead our case, at least."

"No, thanks."

"I won't take no for an answer! We know a shortcut. It's the least we can do."

"You've done plenty already."

I whirled, huffed toward the bay, grabbed the net—not bothering to roll it. "Tubby, hup-two. Get the bucket. We're leaving."

Then, I jogged back up the beach, hurdling the bleacher. "Guys! Wait up!"

Anna turned, holding translucent sandals on her fingers by the straps.

What must I have looked like to her? Sand in my hair. Salt on my cheeks. Wet T-shirt stuck to my skin, stained rust-red beneath my ribs from bloody bluefish battles of yore, wetness seeping up toward my neckline, showing a nipple. Belly button winking at her like a whale eye. The net, hanging over skewed posts in loose, jowly folds. With Tubby, trudging up behind carrying a bucketful of bay.

In that short time, her face had changed. There was a hardness to it. A hint of red over her cheekbones. A gale brewing in her eyes.

"Nick!" she said. "*Please!*"

"I insist," I croaked. "*We* insist."

"On second thought. Anna? Why don't we stay?"

Anna turned, sharply, and looked at Caitlyn. "Huh?"

"I'd hate for them to leave on account of us. They're catching good bait. And they know a shortcut."

"She's got a point," Tubby said, coming up beside me. "One, two more runs, we'll have all the eels we need. And we can still get you guys to the Pancake House before you'd get there yourselves."

"Caitlyn . . . *really?*" She lowered her chin and held Catilyn's gaze. "Our *moms?*"

"Anna," she said, "*Tutrugusustut mume.*"

Tubby blinked. I stood with my mouth slightly open. Anna let out a breath. "Okay," she said. "We'll stay."

"I mean, Anna, are you sure?" I said. "We could walk you right now. It's no problem."

She looked at Caitlyn, who nodded vigorously. "We insist," Caitlyn said.

"Just—make it snappy, would you?"

The girls found their seats. We sprinted down the beach, stretched the net out between us and shook, dropping a few dead inch-longs to the sand. Then, we angled our sticks and waded back into the bay.

"They speak Egyptian now, too?" Tubby whispered.

"God only knows."

"What are we going to do?"

I shrugged. I wasn't totally sure. I had the sense that once we left the bay, I could make a strong case for Kramer's. That I could pretty much fix everything with enough time. There was something niggling in me, though. I felt like I'd always felt when caught in an undertow. Sure, I knew how to swim out. But there was still that initial queasiness, with forces working against you that were hard to fathom.

We walked quietly toward the mussel bed, working purposefully, listening to the soft sound of water lapping against the shore and the far-off hunger cry of a gull. The sun had burned through the haze and a new warmth was creeping into the bay, a half inch at a time. Out in the channel, a bowrider thudded over whitecaps for the Inlet, engine drone rising and falling.

I glanced up the beach. Just as I did, Caitlyn leaned over and whispered something into Anna's ear, shielding her words behind a cupped hand. Anna smiled and nodded, recognition spreading across her face.

I have to give them credit, really. They didn't even flinch until after we'd made the first turn, waist-high in the water. Then, calm as storks in a flood, they stood, snatched their sandals and ran, kicking up sand. Caitlyn said something, raising a quick laugh from Anna, followed by nothing at all.

Tubby and me, we stopped moving, let the net go slack. When we finally dragged our net around the mussel bed and hauled it onto the beach, all we had were clumps of lousy green seaweed. No sand eels. Not even a crab.

We dropped the net and scrambled up the beach, around the bulkhead. There was no sign of them, sight or sound.

We tried one more run after that. Working in silence. Our form was textbook perfect. We knew, though, even before we brought the net out of the water. We'd spooked 'em. Or they'd wised up. The tide had turned. Who ever had a clue where fish went or why they did what they did when they did it?

We shook the net out, rolled it up. Sat side by side for a time on the sloping sand, staring forlornly at the bay.

"This is worse than high tide at Goosebar Sedge," Tubby finally said.

It was just one of those things people said in Bay City, and when they said it, you knew exactly what they meant.

That afternoon, on my dad's boat, we had a tough slog. Anchor or drift. Wreck or channel. Nothing seemed to work. Even the over-the-shoulder trick was for naught. Sea robins and sand sharks—junk fish—kept us busy all day, untangling lines and crows' nests. The pool-winning fluke was barely legal. By the time we started home, Tubby'd worked himself into a froth. *Who do they think they are, ditching us like that?* he said. We were standing next to each other at the aft filleting table, gutting the meager catch, and he was scheming ways to get them back. *We can put a squid in their beach bag . . . or a horseshoe crab in their shower! . . . We can light a bag of fish guts on fire and throw it on their porch!*

"Which do you vote for, Swanny?"

I shrugged. "Anything you want, Tub. It's fine with me."

"Swanny," he said, looking at me stony-eyed with a filleting knife in his hand. "What's wrong with you? Where's your fight?"

"Nothing," I said. "The squid-in-the-bag. That's a great one. Always gets 'em."

What I didn't say was that I seriously doubted we'd ever even see them again. And, anyway, I didn't really blame them. Not like he did.

That night, showered up but still smelling faintly of fish guts, Tubby and I went to Kramer's for the first time that season. The air was sweet with cotton candy and roasted nuts, and Skeeball jackpot alarms pulsed from the arcade. Bumper cars drew fine sparks across a painted night sky in an alternate universe. The dune buggy circled on its track, a little kid gripping the wheel, hair blowing back.

It was as we passed Ring the Bell that I saw her, walking away from us along the sandy rim beside the arcade—wavy blonde hair, tank top, and short shorts—and my heart lifted like a wave over the beach. She disappeared behind a group of passing islanders, then reappeared a boat-length farther away.

She's here, I thought. "They *came!*" I said.

"Huh?" Tubby said.

I opened my mouth to call her name—I'd been secretly hoping

for this, exactly this, all day long out on the open water—and then she turned, and I saw someone I'd never seen before, and all at once, I knew it was over, soup to nuts.

Tubby didn't seem to notice. He whopped me good—"Come on, Nick"—jolting me momentarily back into myself, and we crossed the sandy concourse, lining up behind half a dozen other kids. At the front, we handed over our tickets, clambered into the bucket, yanked the safety bar down.

We rose, and the ground shrank away. Climbed, above the light stanchions, over the hull of the Buccaneer, high into the wind-swept night, until the huge wheel came to a jerky stop. I could see all of Bay City from up there, bay to ocean, Coast Guard build-ing to marina, and what I couldn't get over was how small it all seemed. How little consolation it offered.

A few miles north, the Causeway shot out in a leaping, fluo-rescent arc. To the south, Seaside City brushed the sky orange. Across the bay, pinpricks of light shined weakly through the car-nival haze. The bucket rocked on a breeze. Laughter traipsed up the scaffolding. Giant metal arms cradled us, glowing with light from 5,000 colored bulbs, a beacon to all those at sea.

Then the turbine kicked on and the wheel began to turn, and I started down the other side.

New York

Pulp
and
Paper

Trinity Atlantic Train 109 shimmied through western New York, curving north around Broadbend Mountain, south around Hitch Mine, following a descending range of un-exploded hills toward the Gulch. It moved cautiously, in fits and starts, as if it didn't trust the world beyond its headlights. On Train Trestle Bridge, the 109 attracted the attention of a fisherman a few hundred feet below, wending a spinner through foaming currents. "She was movin' kind of herky-jerky," he said. "She stopped, started, stopped. You could hear noises—shouting. Sound carries pretty good right there, with the rock on both sides. Anyway, she stayed put six or seven casts, then hissed. You had the sense she was packing it in for the night, right there on the Sticks. That prob'ly would've been best, considering."

Eventually, though, the train lurched forward again and seemed to find a purpose. It churned past Rawls Point, through the villages of St. George and Desmond. It glided steadily across Gambler's Ridge on the outskirts of town. A time-lapse photo taken shortly before midnight by an amateur photographer in the valley shows the red lights above the tanker cars as a solid, unwavering line, something you could hang clothing on or feed a phone signal through. The train plunged into Cumberland Forest, agitating a tunnel formed by overhanging beech and sugar maple trees, and, finally, rolled into Slab, crossing the corporation limits at an undemarcated location. City maps show the tracks intersecting the straight-edged eastern border, drawn with ruler and fountain pen by P. Dickson, a surveyor in the office of James Braun & Sons, in 1889, which, as some would later point out—as if it explained something—was the year of the Buffalo flood.

The locomotive's black box recorder indicates nothing amiss at the Peninsula switch, where the 109 veered from the main right of way and went speeding onto the Larsburg Spur; or at the Peninsula substation, where, accelerating, it charged onto the privately maintained tracks of Viridian Pulp & Paper Co. It was there, several hundred yards from the terminus, that the black box detected the first signs of trouble. Just a blip—a subtle decrease in pressure in the air brake control valve. The kind of thing that, when systems were working properly, would self-adjust and rebound unnoticed.

A third-shift worker at Viridian, standing on a bridge four stories high, metering wood chips into a continuous digester, probably had the best view as events unfolded. While the auxiliary dock lights by themselves would not have allowed him to see very much, the center beam of the incoming 109 had a mean luminous intensity in excess of 200,000 candela. Those lights whitewashed six hundred feet of track, conjuring high noon at midnight. From where he stood, he could see the Georgia Southern train, still loaded with roundwood, parked in the debarking bay. And he could watch the 109, on final approach from Parsippany, elongating on the straightaway, its tanker cars barreling through moonlit sawdust.

"I thought I was a goner when I saw that train," he said. "She was comin' in much too fast."

Also, he knew what was in those tankers.

At 12:02 in the morning, Gale Denny was sitting in an easy chair in her den, watching an infomercial for Hercules Hooks, which were designed to hang mirrors, picture frames, and shelves without any tools, but which looked like something you'd use to gaff a muskellunge. The man on TV said they would hold items weighing up to 150 pounds and were easily installed by hand. They came with a free laser level, a $20 value, plus ten bonus hooks, and a thirty-day money-back guarantee. She was seriously contemplating calling the toll-free number. Her sister Libby had given her photos of the kids—three nieces, a nephew, six grand-nieces and grandnephews—that she'd been meaning to hang above the mantle to cover the faded shield where the five-point had hung, but she'd been putting it off. Bill had stored his nails and screws and washers and bolts and rivets and grommets and thingamajigs in jam jars, screwed into jar tops affixed to the base-ment ceiling. There were more than thirty up there, last she'd checked—an easy reach for him, but she needed a step stool. And how on earth was she supposed to know which type of nail to use? Common wire, smooth box, blue lathe, finishing, shingle. He'd talked about nails the way Cousteau talked about oceans: objects of beauty, staggeringly diverse. She envisioned a dozen trips down and up and down again to procure the right ones, the bones of her hip grinding like a mortar and pestle. She saw crooked frames and crumbling drywall. These hooks, though—these Hercules Hooks—all you had to do was push, set, and hang.

She reached over the arm of the easy chair, lifted the receiver.

When she heard the train whistle, she hesitated. She was used to hearing the whistles, of course. The Timber Tracks, as they were known, ran through the woods, a hundred or so yards be-hind her house. She liked the way the whistles revealed a train's personality: angry and churlish; patient and sage; brazen or con-fident or lazy as a bear. It had always been Bill's contention that these "train moods," as she called them, were more a reflection of how *she* was feeling at any given moment than some empirical quality of the sound. But he was wrong. At that moment, for instance, she was feeling annoyed that she was awake again in the middle of the night. The incoming train, on the other hand, with its long, breathy, barrel-chested blast, was tired and lonely, a slump-shouldered giant.

She put the phone down in the cradle, looked across the room, found her reflection in the window.

Bill and she, they'd had a good run. A fifty-year sprint, Bill called it. He never drank to excess. Didn't smoke or chew or gamble and hadn't once been unfaithful. He worked hard, five days a week, the last twenty-two years at Custom Roll Inc., a metal forming company that manufactured framing, channels, rings, and open-seam tubing, rectangular and square, for vending machines, and had retired at age sixty-two with a full pension. She ran the household the way he liked it, paying bills when they came in; cooking with as much cream and cheese and butter as he could want; hanging his laundry on the line behind the house. They never fought. If she wanted to watch the nightly news instead of the Sabres game, he let her, unless the game was close, in which case she let him watch the hockey, unless there was some serious weather coming in, in which case he let her watch the newscast, regardless of the score, unless it was the *playoffs*, which trumped everything up to and including a Perfect Storm. A sprint, Bill called it, though more often, it had felt to her like a marathon.

She turned her attention back to the tube. Maybe now, she thought, closing her eyes. Maybe now . . .

A peal of thunder clapped once above the valley, fracturing her sleep spindles, raising the sense receptors behind her eyes that had finally lain flat. She felt dense and dislocated—had she slept a few hard seconds or half the night?—and she had a skull full of sinkers. She blinked, tilted her head this way and that. She didn't associate the thunder with the train whistle. She just assumed a storm was moving in, exactly the way storms always did at that time of year in her neck of the woods: drawing violence from Erie, zipping across the Allegheny Plateau, barreling over the mountaintops in mushrooming fists. Her first thought, in fact, was surprise that it hadn't stormed earlier, with all that afternoon heat trapped against the hills.

She pressured the footrest down, closing the chair inside itself, then stood and walked out to her back porch. She looked up to see the clouds. To her surprise, there was not a one. The sky brimmed with liquid crystal stars.

Across the field, down the berm and up again, beyond the wild corn patch, an upstairs light glowed at Avery Mayberry's place. Normally, this time of night, Avery's place was dark as dirt. And for good reason. He started work at five A.M. at the hydroelectric plant, a steel and cinder structure out by the dam that turned water into light. She was an old lady, she could be tired as a matter of routine; the world was indifferent. But he operated giant turbine blades that supplied energy at peak hours to a good number of people in western New York. If *he* were tired, people would notice.

At the same time, though—and she was ashamed to admit this—she was glad to know he was up. His was the only house she could see from hers, and, despite the reservoir of open space between them, she felt his presence as company. She liked Avery, almost as much as she'd liked his wife. They'd moved from the city five years before when Avery was transferred. Sarah, game for a change, had taken up gardening as a recreation, growing blueberries, sweet corn, and pumpkins, selling what she could each Saturday at the farmer's market. For four-plus years, they seemed to be enjoying the old farmstead. And then, one Saturday night when Sarah was out of town, Avery got drunk at Doll's Place, slow-danced with Lucy Miller, and took her home to his marital bed. When Sarah told Gale that she was leaving, Gale didn't want to believe it, even though she'd already heard it from her stylist at Beautiful You. It was the kind of thing that happened to the people you read about in *People*. But, as Bill might have told her, what you *want* to believe in this life matters as much as mulch on the Moon.

Gale leaned against a square column supporting the porch roof. Closed her eyes and drew in a small portion of the night. The cool air cleared her head a bit. Soothed her chapped face. She wriggled her toes, felt the chill through the porch boards. She tried to picture a sunny place—Micronesia, maybe, or Guam. She saw some sand, a palm tree. Thatched-roof huts. Bill being Bill, he'd encouraged her to think this way—about what was happening at a point in time on the other side of the earth. He said it would help her remember that even if she felt alone in the middle of the night, she really wasn't. Somewhere, the sun was shining. Commerce was commencing. Always, there was a movie showing, and young people were falling in love.

She heard him before she saw him, and when she turned to look, there he was, standing on the banister at the far end of the porch, flicking his tail in the starlight. "Why, hello there, Fisher." She sat down on the rocking chair and patted her lap. "*Ps, ps, ps, ps, ps*. Did you bring Mama a present?" He looked at her, head level, mouse tail curving from his mouth, then pawed across the banister, bent into his haunches, measured, measured, measured, and jumped, landing silently on the porch boards. He deposited the mouse at the runner, rubbed his ribs against her ankles, and then stretched his gray body up, pawing at her kneecaps. He loaded his springs, leapt onto her lap. "Good boy," Gale said. He purred. Let his head be scratched. She found that spot behind his ear. When he'd had his fill, he jumped down, jawed up the mouse, and legged through a triangular space in the lattice, across the yard toward the forest. *Just like a man*, Gale thought.

It was as she was watching him go that she noticed the fog, stretching fingerlike, from between the trees. In that first instant, it was beautiful. Almost heartbreakingly so. A moment or two later, though, before Fisher disappeared into the trees—before the fog enveloped the shed, facing the hills, and then her gardenias, in the beds—she smelled burnt pineapple. Pepper-flecked and harsh.

Her nostrils flared. Hot aluminum hit the back of her throat. Tears came hard, double-eyes wide. She blinked and squinted, trying to focus.

She knew what'd happened. She'd been worried about it, frankly, ever since Bill died. Al Qaeda had attacked Slab, New York, with chemical, and possibly biological, weapons. She'd imagined it happening so many times, exactly this way.

She rocked up and out of her chair, put her hands on the banister. "Fiiiisher," she called. Fog broke over the verandah, curled around her. "Heeeeeeeere, kitty, kitty." She waited, tried again. Already, her voice grated against the terrorist smell. She turned, hustled into the kitchen. Opened the refrigerator to a cold hum. Found the plate of liver she'd cooked that afternoon, laced into strips. Peeled the Saran Wrap and walked back onto the porch. Padded down to the concrete walk. She couldn't see the cloud anymore, distinctly. She could taste it, though. Feel it working into her chest. Her lips burned.

That's when she heard the second thunderclap, louder than the first, and it drew her attention, hard, to an alien brightness in the lower night sky. Now that she'd heard it again, it didn't sound very thunder-like at all.

Gale held the plate up to the hazed-over night. "Fiiisher," she said. "Heeeeeeere, kitty, kitty. Mama's got treats."

It was as she'd said this last thing that her voice cracked. And, hearing herself—just the slightest quaver, out loud in the dark of night—made her aware of her fear.

It was only the slightest slippage. But panic is the rockslide that starts with a single pebble.

Avery Mayberry had fallen asleep with the lights on. There'd been an outage that afternoon at the plant—he'd spent all day conducting a functional check of the turbine control system, stroking valves, setting valve curves, and verifying trip function in preparation for the restart—and when he finally got home, four hours later than usual, he lay on his bed, fully clothed, toed off his work boots, letting them fall harum-scarum to the floor, and dropped into a powerful, dreamless slumber. He twitched off the first explosion—rolling onto his side, sliding his hands between his knees for warmth. At the sound of the second explosion, he stopped snoring, wet his lips, and yawned, aware, in a distant, dreamlike way, that he was on his bed, still in his work clothes. He let himself drift, one final time. It was the smell that woke him, up and out of his skin.

Viridian, he thought, even before he jerked upright in bed. From his roof, with binoculars, he could clearly see the plant—its "V"-stamped aquamarine water tower; the three chip silos, each with a single window at the base, bound by an elevator that slashed across on the diagonal; the four smokestacks, belching out particulates from the boilers and lime kiln, red lights on top blinking, forever just out of sync, like some enemy code. Some nights, if the wind was wrong, he could smell the hydrogen sulfide. He always feared the plant would kill him one day, either slowly, over time, like the Royal Blunts his father had smoked, or, perhaps, in the blink of an eye, in a terrific ball of chemical fire.

He poured himself out of bed. He could see, through his bedroom window, what looked like a dying fire in the plant's craw and a heavy plume of dark, twisting smoke.

Avery pulled on his mud-crusted work boots and I.B.E.W. Local 41 cap, with the closed fist radiating lightning bolts above the brim. He plucked his backpack from the bottom of the closet and filled it with whatever he could grab as he whirled: flashlight, pocketknife, razor, toothbrush and paste, change of clothes, and dry socks. Already, he was anticipating being out of the house for an extended period of time.

He ran downstairs, taking two, three steps at a clip. As soon as he reached the landing, the smell hit him — on the breeze through an open window above the radiator — and his eyes welled with the sting. Whatever was happening was happening faster than he'd imagined. He jumped the last three steps, flipped on a light, and, breathing into the crook of his arm, bolted into the pantry. He held the knapsack under a shelf and slid two rows of cans — green beans, creamed corn, tuna — over the opening. Several tins hit the floor and rolled. He was struck by an image of his uncle, executor of his estate, finding the errant cans, examining them, piecing together his nephew's last moments on earth.

"Whoa, Nelly," he said. "I'm not dead yet."

Outside, Avery tossed the backpack across the passenger seat of his Marquis, dropped into the car, and backed out, turning up stones. On the street, he threw the car into drive and floored it, tattooing the roadway. Smoke rose in his rearview mirror. He flipped on the radio. First reports of an explosion at Viridian were already coming in, though authorities were urging residents to stay put until further notice. "Stay put, my ass," he said. Then he laughed. He sounded like a stark raving lunatic. Or, as Sarah would have put it: a *stork raven loon 'n chick*. He laughed again, feeling better. Better and better with every inch of road he put between himself and that factory. He took the dip, over the berm, at sixty. Landed hard, felt his ribs shift. It was as he crossed the drainpipe that he saw her in the harsh light glare, rising from a ditch in a nightgown, her hair spreading from her scalp in astral waves.

Avery swerved, nearly clipped her, crossed the oncoming lane, slid into the culvert on the other side. "Mrs. Denny," he said. "Jesus H. Christ."

He knew her, of course. They'd been neighbors five years. He thought of her as a bit of a coot. A recluse, who walked around the house barefoot, muttering to herself.

Sarah had maintained that they'd be coots, too, when they were old. When Bill died, Sarah'd adopted Mrs. Denny as her special project and never ceased reminding Avery that Mrs. Denny had lost her husband of fifty years. "*Fifty years*, Avery," she said. Sometimes, she held up five fingers and a fist for emphasis. She hand-delivered bowls of her choicest blueberries, hauled Mrs. Denny's trash and recycling bins to the curb. Sometimes, Mrs. Denny would catch her at it, and they'd speak, a half hour or more.

Now and again, when Mrs. Denny had a leaky faucet or a stuck window, Sarah would prevail upon Avery to fix it. He always protested. He couldn't stand the smell of her breath over his shoulder—turnip, liver, hot compost. And that damn whiskery cat, scratching those fleas. It made *him* itch.

But Sarah'd smack him, lightly, on the butt, or squeeze his hand, or run her fingers through the short hairs behind his ears.

"Don't do it for me," she'd say, smiling. "Do it for La Grande."

By that, she meant the hydroelectric plant in Quebec, the world's largest, with eight generating stations pumping out more than 16,000 megawatts of power a year, but she meant something else, too, and inevitably, he'd blush, turn his face, and hurry over. Once, he left so fast he forgot to take his tool belt.

Lord Jesus, he thought, backing up onto the roadway, spotting her in his brake lights. *How could I forget Gale?*

He stopped hard, leaned over the passenger seat, pushed open the door. "Mrs. Denny!" He coughed, drew his face tight. "Come on! Get in."

A moment later, she was there, breathing raspy, her hands planted on the front seat. "Avery," she said. "I need your help. I can't find Fisher."

There was something in her eyes he'd never seen before. A bugginess, popped wide from terror and gas.

"Mrs. Denny," he said, slowing himself down, "there was an explosion up at the plant. It's chlorine—you can smell it. We're less than a mile *downwind*. We need to get out of here. Yesterday."

"I'm not going anywhere without Fisher."

"Mrs. Denny," he said, trying again. "I'm sorry about your cat—I truly am . . ." He stopped himself, doubled back. "He's a fighter, though, Mrs. Denny, am I right? Did I not watch with my own eyes when he took out that she-coon?"

He hadn't, actually. He'd heard it, mainly, the horrible yowling, and then heard about it from Sarah, who'd gone out to investigate with a lamp.

"They don't come more resourceful than Fisher. If there's a way to survive, he'll find it. Am I right, or am I right?"

She rubbed fog from her eye. "You're right."

"I'm right!" he said. "He'll find higher ground upwind. He probably already *has*. If you want to live to see him, I'd suggest you get yourself in this car."

Her lower lip trembled. She lifted her hands from the seat, as if she were going to drop down into the car. Her eyes softened, ever so slightly, like smoked ice. *I got her*, he thought. *Thank god almighty, I got her.*

But Gale backed away and bent so she could see him through the window. "Avery," she said. "That's my cat. I'm not going anywhere without him."

He could see, now, in her eyes, the mistake he'd made. What he'd taken for resignation was foreclosure. He didn't know her well, but he knew her well enough to know he had a new choice, and he breathed out hard against it.

"Gale," he said. "I'm going."

She stood motionless in the fog, a figure raised at a séance.

"Have it your way," he said. Then he pulled the door closed, slammed the car into drive, startling the transmission, and hit the gas. He made it beyond her mailbox, then stomped on the brake, locked the tires, and fishtailed to a halt.

It's crazy, how life works. How one minute, you're happy, at peace with your choices—even the worst ones weren't so bad—and then, you do something that can't be undone, and everything you've ever worked toward and wanted is gone. *Poof!* Sayonara.

He could see Gale in his brake lights, hunched in the road. He put his head to the wheel, holding the brake steady with his foot. After a moment, he lifted his head. Sighted her in his mirror. Then he yanked the gear stick down and reversed, swerving, back the way he'd come. From above, it must have seemed as if he were going to run her down—as if his decision had been to put her out of her misery, fast and furious. Only, a car-length away, he screeched to a halt, threw the car in park, stepped out into the swirl, and charged around the tailpipe.

Gale Denny flinched. Held her arm over her eyes.

"Which way did he go?"

"That way." She pointed to the forest beyond her house. "I heard him meowing. Right there. It's just—it's so dark. And he's spooked."

"I'll find Fisher," he said. "Get in the car."

She coughed hard, spat, clutched her robe to her neck. "Please, Avery . . . hurry."

"Leave the car running," he said. "Whatever you do, don't open the vents."

He opened his backpack, took out the flashlight. And then he turned and ran, down the road toward the woods.

Just before he got there, something flickered in the northern sky, and he allowed himself a final glance in the direction of the plant. An orange plume radiated briefly, before fading into darkness. He snorted, shaking his head. Hundreds of employees on three shifts and four black-eyed smokestacks. Giant cauldrons of wood pulp simmering at three hundred fifty degrees. Heavy black liquor and quicklime and chlorine gas. All to make paper. And yet there were wasps—Sarah had told him—that made paper from dead wood and spit. Less than an inch long, he thought, as he slipped between two weeping trees in the vapor, and they'd been doing it that way since the dawn of time.

———

She waited. Held the nightgown over her nose. Coughed through it. Green fog swirled in the headlights. Five minutes passed. Another two. She couldn't breathe. Her house, in the distance, was a ghost ship. She thought about going after him. But she was dizzy, and her toes felt weak. Still, she couldn't just *sit* there.

She shouldered the door open. Needles pricked her eyes. "Heeeeeere, kitty, kitty, kitty," she croaked. Pain strafed her, deep inside. She hauled the door shut. Waved a hand to cool her lips, disperse the gas. She looked back at the house.

For a fraction of a moment, the soundless space between seconds, he was there. Not there, in a vision in her head, but *really* there—just beyond the lit den window, dipping a tarnished rag in Fifty-Fifty, working it over the antlers of his five-point. She could smell the linseed oil and turpentine. And then, she took in a sharp breath, her windpipe tightened, and the house was nothing but a shell.

"Fiiiiiisher," she said. The car door was open again. The air raked her throat. "Heeere kitty, kitty, ki . . ."

Punks rustled beyond the drainage ditch. Her heart started, stopped, started again. She half expected Al Qaeda to emerge from the reeds in gas masks and desert camouflage to take her away at gun point.

"Hello?"

Fisher crashed through the cattails, charged up the berm, bounced onto her lap.

Gale ripped the door shut, sealing them inside, and held him. Pressed him to her bosom. Laid her cheek against the circles of his spine.

"I knew you'd come back," she said. "Fisher, Fisher, Fisher, Fisher."

Fisher hacked, stretching his neck.

She peered through the windshield. The road slithered snakelike from her headlights. There was no sign of Avery, anywhere. *Great*, she thought. "Great, great, great, great, *great*!" She cracked the window, holding Fisher to her chest. Gas hit her face, so noxious, her head whipped back. She clamped her lips, forced herself to turn toward the window. "Aaaaaaaaavery!" She listened. Heard nothing.

She put Fisher, gingerly, on the floor. He protested, but she fended him off with her palm. "Don't worry," she said, "Mama's going to get us out of here."

She climbed over the hand brake, put the car in gear. Drove up the street, parting the fog, and turned onto her driveway, crunching gravel, stopping when she reached the bumper log. Her headlights burned through drifting sheets of cloud. She rolled down the window, far as it went.

"Aaav . . ." A sharp pain guillotined her cry. She heaved up, her neck tight.

After all this—after all this!—if she didn't back out immediately and hightail it to some fresher place, they were both going to die, right there in the front seat. And—maybe *Avery* had found higher ground. You want to talk resourceful, Avery Mayberry was resourceful as hell. *He'll be fine*, she told herself. The best thing to do—the smart thing—was to go find help.

She glanced at her cat. Fisher looked up, a spot of blood foaming under his nose.

Then she put her palms on the horn and leaned. Put her whole body into it. Into that horn she put the aching, all those goddamn years of pain, in her knees and hips and back, aching that ignored pills, chiropractic treatment, and astrological remedy. And she put her sadness, about the man who had come to her door the week after Bill passed and sold her a vacuum cleaner, the most expensive she'd ever owned, which, the second time she used it, made a sound like a busted dirigible and spewed cat hairs through its trap and thereafter never worked a lick. And the toll-free troubleshooting number that she called from the paperwork, which was always busy. Busy, busy, busy, busy, *busy*. Into that horn, Gale Denny put Bill, who ate her pies and cakes and cookies, her stroganoffs and paprikashes, and didn't exercise worth a damn and never would no matter what she said or did or threatened and yet could do a Texas Two-Step as if he'd been born in Laredo instead of Lancaster.

She felt her eyes, felt them burning and going and tearing. She eased off. Rested her palms on the horn. She wanted to honk again—told her hands to sink down, her shoulders to hunch and push—but "again" was too much to ask.

A great silence rose up, a silence as vast and peaceful as a mountain.

Gale closed her eyes. The cat came up on her lap. Arched his spine under her hand. Her fingers touched his hair. His hand. The side of his face.

Big
River

Like her namesake, Garnet was stubborn as hell. So when she turned down my offer to drive her to her first OB appointment—insisting she wanted to go alone—I knew no amount of point-counterpoint could convince her otherwise.

"How're you going to get there?"

"Same way I get everywhere."

By that she meant the bus. Six months after graduating Big River High, Garnet had found a job waiting tables at Gallagher's and moved into a fifth-floor studio at Riverview Apartments, opting to use what savings she had on a security deposit instead of a down payment on a car. She didn't really need wheels. In Big River, it took seven minutes to get anywhere from anywhere else, including from her apartment to mine, a third-floor walk-up above the fossil shop downtown.

In those days, I worked as a field tech for Al's Quality Basements. The Friday of her appointment, not a soul in the North Country was in need of our waterproofing services and time went by like an underwater track meet. Garnet was scheduled to see her doctor at three. I called her apartment at five, left a message, then drove straight home. She hadn't called back, so I picked up one of the pregnancy books I'd checked out of the library, found my page, and started reading. At five thirty, the door chimed on the fossil shop—Dinosaur Dave done for the week. I waited a half hour, closed the book, and picked up the phone, just to make sure it still worked. At seven, I left a second message. Sometime after eight, I retrieved my Louisville Slugger from the back of my closet and began pacing, whacking the bat head into my palm. "Everything's okay," I said, and then, as if the bat had challenged my assertion: "Of course it is!" I left a third message around nine thirty. "I'm really worried, Garnet. Call me. Please." I put the phone down and looked at it, willing it to ring. When it did, I pounced like a bobcat on a snowshoe.

"Garnet! You're home!"

"Hey, Finch."

"Where were you? I called seventeen times."

"I got your messages. I just got back."

"Six hours?"

"I took a walk," she said. "I needed to unwind."

"Unwind why? Is everything okay? The baby's okay?"

"So far, so good."

"Something's wrong. What's wrong?"

"Everything's fine."

"I can tell, Garnet."

She sighed. "Finch. Are we really ready for this? To have a baby?"

"I've been ready the better part of my natural-born life."

"So dramatic," she said. "I mean *ready*."

I could hear the radio in the background. I pictured her sitting on the countertop in the kitchenette, her bare feet swinging. "Because we don't live together."

"There's a good place to start."

"You can move in. We can get married Monday. In City Hall."

"Finch, chill. Would you *chill*? I don't want to get married Monday. This isn't a movie. And besides, what about Strontian?"

She meant the town, in Scotland, where the element strontium was discovered—"Sr" on the periodic table. We had that poster up on the wall in chemistry my senior/her junior year. Strontian was on Scotland's west coast, where the river emptied into the sea. The name came from a Gaelic word meaning "point of fairies," and they had a floating church on the river where Garnet had decided we'd get married one day.

"So we'll wait. We'll tie the knot after the baby comes. We'll leave it with your parents and go to Strontian. How does that sound?"

"You can't just leave a new baby with grandparents, Finch."

A bus rumbled past my window, shaking the glass in its frame. "Garnet?"

"Yeah?"

"I have to ask you. I'm sitting here and all these crazy thoughts are running through my head. You're having this baby, right?"

"That's what the doctor tells me."

"But, I mean, you're not thinking of going to the clinic?"

It was a euphemism. It was the way we all spoke about what Panda Johnson had done after getting knocked up by the rugby player from Frankfurt.

"No, Finch," she said. "I'm having this baby. But I don't want to tell anyone. Not yet."

"We don't have to," I said. "It'll be our little secret."

"'Til I say otherwise."

"'Til you say otherwise."

She sighed again. "I'm seven weeks already."

That's when I finally felt myself start to relax. "Seven weeks! Tell me everything! What'd they say? What happened?"

"They did a bunch of tests. I heard the heartbeat. I'm due in November."

"I'm coming over."

"Not tonight, Finch," she said. "I'm not feeling well."

"I have to see you. I'm bursting."

"I'm nauseous. Maybe tomorrow."

"It's the morning sickness. Too much hCG in your system. You wouldn't believe what's going on inside you. Did you know that right now, the baby has a tail? And webbed fingers. It's floating around in a sac of its own pee."

"Finch," she said, "I gotta go. I think I'm gonna barf."

Garnet was named for the gems that her grandfather, as well as her father and mine, had unearthed from Cooper Mine in the Central Adirondack Mountains. In her grandfather's day, the mine was one of the centers of the garnet industry, not just in New York, but worldwide. When her father first took over as foreman, Cooper garnets were still being shipped on trains and boats and, in some cases, armored vehicles to places as far away as Walla Walla, Washington; Nome, Alaska; and São Paulo, Brazil. It was a Cooper garnet in Princess Grace's tiara when she married Prince Rainier of Monaco, a fact that was a source of pride for no small number of Big Riverians. Last I checked, Ken's Pharmacy was still selling picture postcards of the crown beneath the tagline, "Courtesy of Big River, N.Y."

More than all their flash and dazzle, though, Cooper garnets were among the hardest in the world, and, right up until the mine closed, their primary value was industrial—as replacements for silica in sandblasting, or, crushed down, as an abrasive powder in water jet cutters, which were used in factories across the globe to cut everything from fish sticks to hand tools to titanium. The truth is, for Garnet, *those* stones—the workhorses, not the tourist attractions—were the real source of pride. We'd be installing a ceiling fan in her apartment, and she'd stop and hold the wrench up to the light, admiring the perfect curve of the head and the sharp lines of the shaft, or, maybe we'd be down by the riverside chucking stones into the spin, and she'd hear a sonic boom and look up at a jumbo jet torching through the ether, and she'd say, "Dollars to donuts, that's one of ours," and I always knew exactly what she meant.

I fell in love with Garnet the summer before second grade. My Mom was sick—she'd already started with the butterfly rash on her face, her joints aching, visits to the hospital in Albany—and there were days she couldn't take care of me. On those days, my dad took me with him to work and left me under the watchful eye of Garnet's mom, who ran the front office. We spent that summer prancing around the mine yard not as Finch and Garnet, but as Princess Grace and Prince Rainier, or Pocahontas and Captain John Smith, or Lady Lizard and Sir Salamander. We hunted arrowheads and fossilized insects in the riverbank and stored them in empty file-cabinet drawers in the back office.

We also played hide and seek in the woods bordering the mine—the finder earning the right to pick through the findee's stash of stones. Sometimes, it would take me an hour or more, weaving through bending birch and sudden beech groves, to find Garnet, wedged, stock-still, inside a fallen tree or tucked behind the sticks of an abandoned beaver dam.

Once, near the end of summer, I hid in a sandy groove in the riverbank, scooped out by high water, beneath the roots of a prehistoric fir. It was a great spot. From the slope leading to the water, it looked like the river was flush with the shore. The first time Garnet approached, she was singing to herself—"Heeeeere, Finchy, Finchy, Finchy"—chipper as a ground squirrel in a field of corn nuts. Fifteen minutes later, though, when she came by again, she was silent, stalking determinedly across the river bank. It was twenty minutes or more before she came back. I heard her frustration—a sigh borne on held hot air—and, frankly, I was cold and bored out of my skull. So I reached up and snapped a tree root. She stopped walking. A moment later, she jumped down onto the sand and crossed her arms. Right there, with the river racing around her, she said she didn't want to play for arrowheads any longer. She wanted to play for kisses.

"Not in a million years."

"It's the new rule," she said. "Starting now. You got found. You owe me one."

"You changed the rules."

"No rule said I couldn't."

She crab-crawled over and presented her lips.

"Not fair!"

"It's the rules," she said. And before I knew what the hell I was doing, I kissed her, on the mouth, the moss over the tree roots grazing our hair.

In fifth grade, we officially became boyfriend and girlfriend, but by then, all it meant was that I got to walk her home from school and hold her bookbag and she could write my name in her notebook with a heart over the "i." At Big River High, we were best friends. She dated a lot, mainly older guys, never me. The summer before her junior year, she fell in love with her Spanish tutor, a volunteer from the International Center downtown. She was "deliriously happy," she said. And then one night, two weeks before the homecoming dance, she phoned me in tears. The Spaniard had broken it off.

I went to her house to cheer her up. We sat together on the edge of her bed. He had taken her out to Cocono's, she said. She thought it was a regular date, but when the salads arrived, he told her he didn't love her the way she loved him. He respected her too much to keep dating. "Is that what we were doing? *Dating*?" She sighed from the back of her throat. "I sat through an entire dinner holding it together after being *dumped*." When she teared up, I moved my arm over her shoulders. "I'm such a moron."

"You're not a moron, Garnet. The Spaniard's the moron."

She laughed lightly, smiled. "He's from Milwaukee." Then she lifted her head and looked at me. Her hair was brook-trout brown, short, straight, evenly bobbed, and her eyes were flecked like the bottom of the river at high noon on the sunniest day of the year. When I kissed her, our top teeth clinked. "Softer," she said. "Like this."

"Your parents . . ." I worked to untuck her shirt.

"Not home." She held her arms straight up.

We slept together on her childhood bed. It was my first time, not hers. I remember looking up with her underneath me and seeing Strawberry Shortcake stickers on her wooden headboard, tapping back and forth against the wall. She had tried to peel a couple off, leaving just the backings—gauzy moons with angular clouds drifting in. After, she cracked her window, lit a cigarette, and sat, naked, on the bed.

"Strawberry Shortcake, huh?" I nodded at the headboard. I knew all those characters from my kid sister, Ava.

She blew a plume out the window. "What about it?"

"Oh, nothing."

"No, you started it—what?"

"A little old for that, aren'tcha?"

"Sue me," she said. "I'm a girl."

"I mean, Ava has a whole book of Care Bears, if you're out."

"Don't you dare." She stuck a finger between my ribs, and I drew back. "You'll stop right there if you know what's good for you."

"I may be able to rustle up some Monchichis. I could look into it."

It happened in a flash—the cigarette on the windowsill, her leg swung over, straddling me. She pinned my wrists up with one hand and started tickling the crap out of me with the other. I caught her hand and flipped her hard, a rodeo calf. And then we really went at it, Hulk Hogan meets Rowdy Roddy Piper in Garnet's bedroom, headboard slamming the wall. Make no mistake: she was strong as hell.

"Betty Crocker!" I managed. She had worked herself back on top of me, and I was struggling to keep track of her hands. "We could get you an Easy-Bake Oven."

"Hmm, what do we have here?" She took a hand away, raised up her hips, reached down. "Looky who's joined the party. Didn't think we'd see him back again so soon." She leaned over me—breasts barely brushing my chest—opened a bedside drawer, pulled out another condom. She slipped me back inside of her one-handed, and we went at it again, the air charged with nicotine from her cigarette.

We were together uninterrupted after that, going on three years, except for one week my senior year when she got mad at me for telling her Ava was at a friend's house when in fact she was home, in her room, adjacent to mine. We messed around an hour solid. When we finished, Garnet got up to pee and found Ava listening at my door with her ear against a Dixie cup. What were those noises, Ava wanted to know. She craned her head so she could see me, lying in bed with the sheets pulled up, and I waved at her. Was there a pig in there? Garnet put a hand on her shoulder and walked her down the hall. There were no barnyard animals, she explained. What Ava'd heard was a natural and safe part of adult life. But Ava wasn't satisfied. If Garnet didn't tell, she was going to ask Dad. You can't ask your father, Garnet said. Then tell me. Garnet said she couldn't—not just then—but she would,

when Ava turned sixteen. That's so far! Ava said. So Garnet told
her about promissory notes. She found a napkin in the bathroom
and wrote:

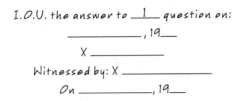

She had Ava write in the date of her sixteenth birthday, then
signed it, marched down the hall, ordered me to sign and date it.
She told Ava to present it on her sixteenth birthday and Garnet
would be obligated to explain everything, right then and there.
Frankly, Ava seemed pretty proud just to have such a thing in her
possession. Garnet ruffled her hair, kissed her on the forehead,
gathered her things, and stalked out, letting the door slam behind her.

For a week, she wouldn't even take my calls. And then one
night, I phoned for the umpteenth time, and, miracle of miracles,
she picked up.

"You knew she was home," Garnet said.

"Sue me," I said. "I'm a boy."

"Do it again—lie to me with a straight face—and the wed-
ding's off."

"Okay okay okay."

But I didn't really believe her. By that time, Garnet and me,
we were like Big River after it's collected all that winter runoff
from Jones Creek and Moose Drink Stream, made the wide turn
around Big Bend, and funneled into the gorge. We had our ups
and downs, but we'd loved each other since Lady Lizard and Sir
Salamander.

What the hell could stop us?

She wasn't feeling any better Saturday. On Sunday, she went
with her parents to visit her cousin in North Elba. Monday, I took
Ava ice skating at WinterFreeze, which I'd been promising to do
for several eons. Tuesday, before her shift, Garnet volunteered at

the Food Bank, sorting cans and dry goods from the various drop-off points around town. Wednesday, all day, it rained like hell and the river rose up and we had half a dozen emergency calls. I spent the next few days wading through flooded basements, cutting drains in concrete floors, laying PVC pipe, installing our patented B-Dri system. It wasn't unheard of for Garnet and me to go four or five days, even a week, without seeing each other, but this time, as I drove spacers into mason walls and hung sheets of shielding, I missed her to the point of distraction.

Garnet phoned Sunday evening. She had a yen for lemongrass chicken and crispy vermicelli noodles. Could I come over and stop off at Saigon Dragon on my way? My heart pounded as I rode the elevator up to the fifth floor.

"Hey." She leaned up, kissed me on the lips, took the plastic bag. "Oh, God, I'm soooooooooooooooo hungry."

If you didn't know her, you never would have been able to tell. But I could. Something about her face, a kind of subtle roundness, the difference between a boulder in the river and that same boulder in the river after fifty years.

We sat on the rug across from each other at her coffee table and ate with chopsticks, right from the cartons. She slurped noodles and drank Diet Coke, talked about her shift the previous night. Stupid Lime had played, and all the groupies showed up from Poughkeepsie. I told her about Ava, how she'd met some boy at WinterFreeze, and he'd asked her out on center ice. Garnet had sextillion questions. Did she like him? Was he nice? Was he *cute*? I described him for her, as best I could.

"I'm stuffed." She put her chopsticks down, hung her jaw as if she were out of breath. "Couldn't eat another grain."

She looked at me and smiled.

"Good," I said. "I have something for you."

"You do?" She tilted her head. "What?"

I stood, went outside into the hallway, returned with the leather case I'd left beside her door. I pushed aside the cartons, put the case on the table, and flipped it open. "It was my grandfather's. A two hundred by fifty millimeter refractor. It's an Alvan Clark & Sons—an oldie but goodie."

She looked at the telescope nestled next to a collapsible tripod, then back at me.

"Go ahead," I said. "It's yours."

"What for?"

A few weeks before my mom died—she couldn't walk at all by then—she called me to her bedside and told me I was a survivor—I'd be fine without her—but just in case, if I ever really missed her, I should take something I truly loved and give it to someone I cared for. If you do that, she said, I'll be near you. I was ten. I didn't understand. I remember thinking about giving up my baseball cards or my S.S. Enterprise deck. What about Ava? I said. Sure, Mom said, smiling. You can give it to Ava. No, I said. I mean—can I give *Ava* away. Mom laughed so hard, she cried.

"No reason. Just because."

She reached over and plucked the telescope from the dark velvet folds. "Finch. I can't take this."

"Sure you can."

"It was your grandfather's."

"It mostly sits in the closet. I want you to have it. *He'd* want you to have it."

Something turbulent came into her chin the way it sometimes did. I could see her struggling against it. "I'll borrow it."

I shrugged. "Call it what you want. I'm not asking for it back."

I led her out to the balcony. It took me a few minutes to set it all up. When I finished, I tipped the scope up toward a three-quarters moon rising above the river, stepped back, and held out my hand. "Take a peek."

Garnet bent, put her eye to the eyepiece, sucked in a sharp breath. "Oh, God, Finch," she said. "It looks . . . it's so—*actual.*"

"I know."

"You can see—there's like, an *ocean* or something—"

"The Sea of Tranquility."

"—and craters. Hundreds of 'em." She steadied the scope with both hands. "You can see *shadows*. It's got—*texture!*"

"Yup."

She looked at the moon for a long while, aiming just so. "I wonder where they put that flag," she said. "Armstrong and those guys."

"You're looking at it."

She worked the focus. "Gives me goose bumps."

I showed her how she could point it off into space, searching for stars and planets. *Look at this!* She said. And, *Finch, quick—I think I found a meteorite!*

"You know," I said. "There's a time capsule out there, some-where. Floating through space."

She slid the telescope across the cosmos. "What's that?"

"My grandfather told me about it. You know Carl Sagan? The astronomer? He made a record with all these messages from planet Earth, and then they sent it off into deep space for extraterrestri-als to find. So they'll know about us."

She backed off and looked at me, hands on her hips. "Nuh uh."

"Yeah huh!"

"You're teasing."

"Swear to God! They put all kinds of stuff on it. Sounds from nature—surf, wind and thunder. Birds, whales—you name it. Plus, there's greetings from Earthlings in like fifty languages. A mariachi band. Even Chuck Berry."

"They really think there's an E.T. out there somewhere?"

"Strong possibility."

"How do they know the aliens will find it?"

"They're hedging their bets."

"How do they know the aliens'll be able to *play* it?"

"It comes with instructions."

"What if they can't understand them?"

"Well, I don't know about that. These guys who did it, Sagan—he's pretty smart. I don't think he'd waste his time unless he was pretty sure the aliens could figure out the instructions."

"We should've sent a record player." She reached for her pack of Camel Lights.

I caught her wrist, hard. "What're you doing?"

Garnet's face, when she was angry, was the flint-lit strike face of a hammer, rearing up. "What's it look like?"

"Your doctor said it's okay?"

"My doctor's not having this baby." She worked her wrist free. "I am."

"You should think about the baby."

"You should mind your own business." She popped a Bic, thumbed the sparker, took a deep drag, blew the smoke up be-tween her eyes.

"Garnet," I said. "I'm just—concerned. For your well-being."

"Oh? For mine?"

"Both."

"Jesus, Finch. One cigarette's not going to kill anyone. My Mom smoked the whole time I was in utero. I turned out okay." She hit the sky with a smoky, Jericho blast.

I nodded. In one of my books, though, it said smoking deprives babies of oxygen and decreases birth weight. There was a photo of a stillbirth. I'd show it to her. She'd come to her senses.

We stood there not speaking for awhile, Garnet apart from me, arms crossed.

"You know," I said, "one of the things they have on that record is a mother shushing a crying baby."

She scoffed. "That's dumb."

"Why? It's not dumb."

"Because it's *stressful*." Her words came out over the smoke. "We're communicating with E.T. Why the hell do we want to stress him out?"

"It's not stressful, Garnet. It's human."

"Easy for you to say."

"What?"

"Just wait and see."

I rolled my eyes up at all that dark matter. "Yeah, well, I wouldn't worry too much about it. Grandpa said it'll take forty thousand years for the capsule to approach the nearest planetary system. So, thirty thousand, nine hundred eighty-nine years to go."

She pinched the cigarette, sent it pirouetting down toward the river on a rind of gray vapor. "Or about thirty-two weeks," she said, "depending on how you see it."

For a week, I steered clear of pregnancy talk, but the strain wouldn't quite go away. It was there in the edge of her voice when we spoke on the phone. I felt it when she didn't reach for my hand walking down Main Street.

Friday night and into Saturday, a cold front dropped down from Quebec and it snowed, and Saturday afternoon, we met at Java Zone for hot chocolate. The whole time we were there she seemed distracted, carving her initials in her whipped cream with a stirring straw, always looking up when the door chimed and someone came in. We weren't there a half an hour when she said she needed to go to get ready for work.

Outside, our breath was white and the sky was flat and the light was the muted light at the mouth of a mineshaft. We walked through the outside seating area with iron tables chained to the gate and green plastic chairs stacked in the corner, a dusting of snow over everything. I stopped to tie my shoe.

"Hey," she said. "Come here a sec. Check this out."

She stood in front of a splintery wooden telephone pole next to the bike rack that hadn't been unbent since the snowplow incident. Hundreds of old staples spread up the pole like a rash of mosquitoes, their backs glinting purple-white streetlight. A flier advertised a used futon for twenty bucks, with pull-off phone number tags at the bottom; another featured a black and white photo of a pointy-eared dog, a Lone Ranger kerchief around its neck, offering "reward for return of beloved family pet."

"You've seen Fritz?"

"That one." She pointed to a flier stapled to the far side, its edges fluttering:

Are you Tired of the
Same Old Thing?
Want to
MAKE A DIFFERENCE
In this world?
Come Learn About
Global Action Corps
And find out <u>How</u>

"Have you seen this before?"

I shook my head. Fritz and the futon had been up there beating back rain, sleet, and snow for a while, but this one was new.

"Have you heard of this—Global Action Corps?"

"Nope—never."

She reached into her purse, pulled out her calendar, jotted down the details. "It sounds interesting, doesn't it?"

Garnet had, once or twice in passing, broached the idea of becoming a Peace Corps volunteer, but as far as I knew, she'd never pursued it—even so much as sent away for information—and I'd never taken it seriously. "Not particularly."

"To me it does."

"Sounds like some hippie dippy thing."

"It's at the *college*."

"Like I said."

She put the calendar back in her purse. Her eyes were shiny and cold, itchy with something bright. "Finch—come on! We should go!"

"Not my cup of tea, Garnet."

"Which part?"

"Oh, I don't know. Global. Action. Corps."

"I don't want to go alone."

"Why not?"

"It's at the *college*." She put her hands up like claws and sidestepped in place. "I vant to suck your bloooooooooood."

"You're a big girl," I said. "You can handle yourself."

"Pleeeeeeeeeeeeeeeze, Finch," she reached up, pinched my earlobes between her thumb and index knuckle, and sweetly waggled them. "Pretty please with honey on top."

"What's in it for me?"

"I'll take you to Swenson's. Buy you a Double Deluxe—with fries."

"I don't know."

"And a frosty!"

I sighed, but I was capitulating, and she knew it. "You drive a hard bargain."

"Yippee!" She hopped up and down, clapping like a cheerleader. "Jesus, Mary, Mother of God, what am I going to wear?"

———

She still had pretty bad morning sickness. But as the week progressed, Garnet's mood seemed to lift, steadily, like the gondola at Caribou Peak. Thursday night, I put the pregnancy book inside my jacket pocket and went to Gallagher's. Garnet stood at the bar flip working on a check. She saw me, waved, held a finger in the air.

I went to our booth, took a load off. Ten minutes later, she brought me a Saranac I.P.A. and slid across the bench. In the dim light, I could see faint pebbles of acne sweeping up from her chin on the left side. Chapter three: hormones wreaking havoc on sebaceous glands.

We made small talk. Ava was officially dating that guy from WinterFreeze, and Garnet couldn't get enough details. Get me a picture, she said. ASAP! At one point, she got up to help package a take-out order. When she returned, she put a highball glass on the table, sipped through a straw.

"Ahhhhhhhhhhhhhh," she said. "This stuff'll put hair on your chest."

"What's your pleasure?"

"Lime juice, Diet Coke, shot of grenadine," she said. "One hundred percent, FDA approved, baby safe."

"Atta girl." I shifted, felt the book pressing into my ribs. "Hey, speaking of which—I wanted to talk to you about something." I pulled out the book, placed it on the table between us. The stillborn photo was bookmarked with a Tuff-N-Dri lifetime guarantee card. "I've been reading this stuff—about the baby. Fetal development."

She put her lips together and nodded. "Whatcha got?"

"Like—okay, check this out. The baby's ears won't be structurally complete for another fifteen weeks, give or take. But he—"

"Or she."

I smiled. "Or she—can already hear us. Even now. By picking up vibrations in her skin and bones."

"Radical."

"It is!"

"So the fetus can hear us, huh?"

"And pretty soon, *react*. It'll hear something from outside, and its heart rate'll go through the roof."

"Which raises a question. What do we *tell* it?"

"Huh?"

"This is critical, Finch." She sipped her spritzer. "What we have here is literally a once in a lifetime opportunity to make a first impression."

I rocked back against the bench. "Well, I don't know," I said. "I wasn't thinking of it that way."

She raised her eyebrows and tapped her temple, as if the idea had originated there.

"What should we say?"

"Maybe we should tell it a joke."

"I like that approach. I like where you're going with this, Garnet. Start the baby off with humor. Got any good ones?"

"How do you get a hundred dead babies in a Volkswagen?"

A laugh shot out my nose, despite myself. "How?"

"La Machine."

"You're horrible," I said. "A horrible, awful person. And sick. Why did the dead baby cross the road?"

"Why?"

"Stapled to the chicken."

She stretched her face tight and nodded. "What's funnier than a dead baby?"

I mock concentrated, scratching my chin, looking up at where the lamp chain met the ceiling. "What?"

"A dead baby in a clown costume."

I laughed. "Then again, maybe we shouldn't."

"No, prob'ly not."

She swung around, pressed her back against the wallpaper with the repeating compass pattern, put her feet on the bench, and drew her knees in. "I have an idea."

"Shoot."

"Why don't we just say: 'We look forward to meeting you'?"

I clamped my lips down against a smile. "'We look forward to meeting you.'" I sipped my beer. "That could work."

She tapped her frontal lobe again. "What else you got in that big book of yours?"

"Well . . ." I started. She swirled a few cubes in the bottom of her spritzer. She wasn't drinking booze. I hadn't seen her light up since that night on the balcony. And that stillborn photo—it was bound to upset her. I drew the book back across the table, slipped it into my jacket pocket. "That was the main thing, I'd say. We got that out of the way. That pretty much covers it."

The incredible thing was just how many people there were, looking for something to save. At least fifty in the lecture hall, most of whom I didn't know—college kids, professor types—but a few of whom I did. Clem Haskins, who owned the Dew Drop Inn, leaned on the stage like he owned it, gesturing to Ellery Bea, who made change at the Laundromat. Syl Todd, wife of Big River's dentist, was there with her kids—two girls and two boys running up the center aisle, slipping around a slide projector, then across the back, down the sides, up again. Two-thirds of Stupid Lime was there—Palko and Tyler, lead singer and bass guitarist. We took a seat three-quarters back. Garnet sprinkled waves here and there. *Hi!* she mouthed. *Good to see you!*

At precisely eight-oh-one, the rear doors opened, and a man in a sports coat came loping down the center aisle. When he reached the front, he placed his briefcase on stage, planted his palms, and pressed himself up. Then he dusted his jeans and looked out at the audience. What struck me was how young he seemed—with his foppish mop of curly black hair and anthracite eyes. He might have been younger than me.

"Wow," I said. "Boy Wonder."

"Shhhh," Garnet said, curtly, and, except for the Todd kids, the place fell silent.

"Thank you all for coming," he said, after a moment. "I hope you're all here for the Transcendental Meditation Session."

The way Garnet laughed, you would have thought it was open mic night at the Comedy Hut.

"I'm Riley Holt, executive director of Global Action Corps. You can call me Riley." He paused, flashed a smile that was a cross between J.F.K. and Jesse James, twinkling with stardust. "Wow—what a turnout. I can't tell you how encouraged I feel when I see a turnout like this. I have the best job in the world."

I cast a sideways glance at Stupid Lime, hoping to catch Palko's eye. But Palko watched the stage, intently.

Riley began to pace. Global Action Corps, he said, was a service organization—a shorter version of the Peace Corps, offering stints of three, six, and nine months, and a year. They placed volunteers all over the world, from Tanzania to the Australian outback, the Pacific Islands to Mexico City, helping victims of poverty, famine, and ethnic strife. Volunteers worked on everything from economic development to rural health projects, fending off dysentery and malaria. "I could go on and on," he said. "But you can get all this from the brochure. What I really want is to tell you my story."

He jumped off the stage, and Garnet rocked back, ever so slightly, as if she'd been blasted by his energy field.

"I'm from Smytheville, PA," he said, pacing again, back and forth between the front row and stage. "Anyone know it? Yeah? It's small. Smaller than Big River.

"I guess you could say I was one of those Mr. Everythings that everyone hates in high school. Quarterback. Track captain. Debate champ. I graduated Smytheville High with a four-point and accepted a full ride to Princeton. First Smytheville kid ever to get in. I was pretty famous in my town. They had a spaghetti dinner send-off for me at the Elks." He looked straight up at the ceiling thirty feet above. "I can't tell you how many people patted me on the back that night. I signed two dozen autographs—not just for kids: World War Two vets. Housewives. The mayor. One guy came up to me and acted out the final play in the championship game against Polk. *Holt under center . . .*" He stopped pacing between the sections and bent, as if about to receive a snap. "*Steps back in the pocket. Looooooking. Looooooooooking. He's got a man down the right sideline!*" He cocked his arm and unleashed a bomb toward the back corner of the hall.

"You can bet I thought I was holy hot shit, pardon my French. I rolled into Princeton with the world at my feet. Only, funny thing happened when I got there. Everyone there had thrown the game-winning touchdown against Polk. And more. Much more. My roommate had appeared on Broadway. Kid in my bio class was working on a cure for Gaucher's disease. All I'd achieved, all those things that seemed so important, didn't amount to a hill of beans. And if none of that mattered, what did?"

Garnet sat posture perfect, hardly daring to breathe.

"I went into a tailspin. I drank. Smoked way too much dope. And then one day, I went on a bender with a couple of kids from my floor. Hit three bars before lunch. Don't remember much, tell the truth. Fell asleep on a bench in front of fountain. Like this." He ran toward the stage and leapt on, triple-jump style, then lay down, knees up, neck tipped back, and started snoring.

Garnet laughed, nervously, a giggle that caught and spread.

"When I woke," he said, "there was a flier in my mouth, rolled up. My head pounded. My throat felt ripped apart and sewn back together. I just assumed it was a joke. I shoved the flier in my pocket and forgot it. Later, I was heading out for some pizza and found it again. Could someone hit the lights?"

There was a scurrying in the rear, and the room went black, save for the sharp white light, wafering through the projector grate. Riley clucked the slide. There, on screen, twenty feet wide by ten feet high, was the flier we'd seen on the telephone pole.

"You can still see the teeth marks," he said.

Riley'd phoned the number on the flier. The recruiter who had placed it in his mouth met him at the pizza place. Apologized. But said he was disgusted that so many kids with so much did so little for so long—wasted their lives partying—and when he saw Riley there on the bench, he couldn't help himself. Six weeks later, Riley was on a plane to Mauritania, helping to stabilize sand dunes and stave off desert encroachment.

Riley clicked through the slides. There were pictures of black women with flies in their hair stooped over cooking pots. There were huts and bonfires, white volunteers reading picture books, a tiny black hand holding a spade. The last picture was Riley Holt, tanned and slim, carrying a little black girl in a flowery dress, her arms draped around his neck, a black boy clamped to each leg.

"Lights!" he said—and they blasted on, whitewashing the image.

"That last picture was taken in Ghana, where I fell in love." He nodded at the kids. "I did six months there, working in Prampram, a tiny seacoast village. These people have none of the things we take for granted—dental care, eyeglasses, running water. But the kids—they're the happiest kids I've ever seen." He looked up at them again, then back at us, shaking his head at the wonder of it all. "The village goes by the traditional name, 'Gbugbla,' which means: 'Keep on trying,'" he said. "Can you imagine that? A town named not for an explorer or colonialist—not even for a natural landmark—but for a fundamental human aspiration?"

I caught Garnet just then out of the corner of my eye. She brought a quick knuckle up, rubbed her mascara, stretched her face tight, and let out a hard breath, fending off something quavering and unpredictable rising up inside her. I looked away, stared at the wooden seat before me, where J.T. had carved a proclamation of undying love to B.L.

Riley Holt was offering more than just redemption. He was holding out the very prospect of a meaningful life. The thing was, I didn't care. Not about desert encroachment in Mauritania or poor kids in Gbugbla or anywhere else. I cared about Garnet, and the family we were starting, right there in Big River. That was more than enough. What hit me, sitting there in that sloping auditorium, was that for Garnet, maybe it wasn't.

"Global Action Corps changed my life," Riley said. "And it could change yours, too. Thank you very much for your time."

There was a surge toward the stage, like so many minnows to a balled piece of bread. I told Garnet I'd wait for her outside and watched as she drifted down with the rest of them.

In the car, I rolled down the window, adjusted the rearview so I could see the building behind me. The college station was playing Metallica, but I wasn't in the mood, so I found an NCAA hockey game from New Hampshire. I fiddled with the heat vents, checked my watch. "Five more minutes. By the clock." A gaggle of students walked under a streetlight, hanging out above the wind-shield—glommed together, laughing like cockatoos. I huffed and puffed and blew hot air at my graduation tassel, dangling from the mirror. A few minutes later, I clicked the radio off and pushed the door open, but just as I did, the passenger door opened. Garnet dropped down and smiled.

"Hey." I yanked the door shut. "I thought I lost you."

"There was a huge crowd. I couldn't get a word in edgewise."

I put the car in drive, but Garnet's hand came out and landed on mine. "A bunch of folks are going to the Zone. I was thinking I'd go, too."

"Who—*Riley*?"

"And a bunch of other people. Palko's going."

"Garnet, you're not seriously thinking about doing this, are you?"

"Why not?"

"You can't just up and go to Mauritius or whatever. You have a job."

"I'm tired of my job."

"You're *pregnant*."

Her hand dropped to my knee. "They have short programs. Three months. Some are close. There's one in Nova Scotia. Another in the Bahamas. We could both go. I could work with the banana farmers, and you could learn how to navigate by the stars. Finch, we're so young. And there's so much good we can do for this world."

"I don't suppose there's a lot of work for basement waterproofers down there."

She brought her hand to her lap. "You think I'm crazy."

I turned and looked at her face, lit golden by the streetlight.

Once, we were gemstones. In the storeroom, in the back office, there was a heavy blanket. Garnet would go in, shut the lights, and wrap herself up. I'd come along with an invisible rock chisel, break through, and find her with a flashlight: a still, huddling ball. She'd protest if I didn't make a good show of it, with action and sound effects—*chink, chink, chink, ca-chink, chink, chink, chink, ca-chink*—removing all that strata. Bit by bit, I'd uncover her. Maybe the first thing I'd see would be the concave space beneath her ankle or the freckle atop her ear. *Chink, chink, chink, ca-chink*. And then, with a final blow—*chunk . . . ker-chunk*—I'd yank the blanket back, and there she'd be: wide-eyed in the sudden glare, lashes dipping down, freshly exposed to the wonder of the world.

"No," I said, "you're not crazy. You're right. You should go."

"I should?"

"Yeah—sure. You might learn something."

"That's what I was thinking."

"You never know what you'll pick up."

She bobbed her head up and down, eyebrows arching confirmation. "What about Swenson's?"

I shrugged. "We'll go another time."

She smiled, and her hand moved back to my knee. "You wanna come?"

It wasn't the same. It wasn't: Come.

"Nah—I'm actually kind of beat. Can you get a ride?"

She touched my cheek with the back of four fingers. "Okay," she said, pushing the door open. "I'll call you later."

She stepped out, shut the door, ran for Schaeffer Hall. I watched her recede in the rearview. When she reached the edge of the lot, though, she stopped, one foot on the curb, one foot off, and stood for a moment like the pedestrian in midstride on the crosswalk sign, snared in time. Then she turned, bolted back to the car.

"Otherwise," she said.

"Huh?"

"*Otherwise.*"

That's when I remembered our conversation, after her OB appointment. "You're—ready? To start telling people?"

She looked at me and smiled—not with her lips, exactly—mainly with her eyes and her cheeks and a little bit of her nose.

"I'm ready," Garnet said.

I didn't go back to my apartment right away. I drove around awhile, hydroplaning on skids of moonshine, thinking about how to break the news to our parents. When Garnet got back from the Zone, we'd call our folks, tell them we had an announcement. Gather at her parents' place. This was the first grandchild on either side. We had to come up with something good. I stopped off at Big River Pizza for a slice. Sat on one of the wooden benches beneath the map of Italy with the tourist sites drawn in. Nothing came to me though. I finished eating, got back in my car. Up ahead on Main, the pharmaceutical gleam of Ken's slapped the sidewalk fluorescent.

They had exactly one relevant greeting card—"You're Going to Be Grandparents!"—with a potpourri of pencil-sketched baby paraphernalia: booties, rattle, bottle; a yellow duckie in a heart. Inside it said: "Very soon, you'll be able to say, 'Ask me about my new grandchild!'" I took the card and the envelope behind it. Somehow, though, it didn't seem big enough. At the end of the aisle, I surveyed the postcard racks. They had the usual fare: Princess Grace's tiara; Cooper Garnet Mine; plus, for the campers, a selection of wildlife cards—pine marten, house finch, olive-sided flycatcher. I spun the racks. When they stopped spinning, three cards I'd seen dozens of times before popped out at me in a whole new way, like a jackpot at Indian Ridge.

At home, I cut a piece of blue construction paper in half and pasted it over half a pink piece. Next, I cut out the phrases and words I needed from the cards and pasted them onto the paper:

You're Going to Be Grandparents!

Courtesy of

Garnet *and* finch

When I finished, I held the paper out in front of me, admiring my handiwork. It was goofy as all hell. Garnet was going to love it.

The phone rang as I was cleaning up paper scraps.

"Finch!"

"Garnet! I was just thinking about you. I think I finally outdid myself . . ."

"I need to see you."

Her voice sounded as if it were coming through a paper shredder. "What . . . Is everything okay?"

"I need to talk to you. Can you come over?"

"It's that guy, right?"

"What guy?"

"That Global Action guy. What'd he do?"

"It's nothing like that."

"I'll kill him, Garnet. I swear to God I will."

Her voice edged up. "Finch! Please—can you just come? *Please?*"

I ignored the red light at Main and Moonachie, clipped the curb at Water Street, sent my homemade card sliding off the passenger seat and onto the floor. I didn't bother waiting for the elevator, taking the stairs two, three at a clip. I pounded her door like a firefighter emptying a house on fire.

Her eyes were red-rimmed, her lips sandbar-parched. She had changed into the pajamas with the floating cow heads. Even then, if you didn't know just how to look, you would have missed that she was pregnant.

"Hey," she said, gesturing to the couch. "Sit." There was an ashtray with half a dozen cigarettes smoked to the filter. She'd recently finished one. I could still smell it.

"What's going on, Garnet?"

"Please, Finch, sit. You're making me nervous."

"*I'm* making *you* nervous." I followed her hand, dropped onto the plaid sofa, sloughed off my jacket.

"Drink?"

"What happened, Garnet?"

She sighed, took a seat in the matching chair, catty-corner, inched up as far as she could, put her elbows on her knees, and meshed her fingers together. She looked tired, but calm, as if whatever storm had hit her had spun her around and passed right through.

"We went to the Zone," she started. "Six of us, plus Riley. We pushed those three round tables together. Riley asked us to introduce ourselves. Where we're from. What we do. Our major. That kind of thing. Palko talked about the band and the summer tour. That time in Athens when that girl came up on stage. There was this kid Alberto who had done his junior year in Colombia. Another guy built houses in Marrakech. I'm sure it was all fascinating. The whole time, though, I couldn't focus. I kept thinking about telling our parents—about the baby. Trying to imagine the words coming out." She rubbed her kneecaps. "I should've felt happy. But I didn't. I felt sick."

"Morning sickness."

"It wasn't that."

"How do you know?"

"I know."

"You're nervous, Garnet. Me too. It's a big deal."

She shook her head slowly back and forth.

I picked a piece of lint off the cushion and began rubbing it between my fingers.

"So it comes to me. 'I'm Garnet,' I say. 'I'm a waitress.' But nobody says anything, so I say: 'I'm from Big River.' Is that funny, Finch?"

"Not to me."

"Me either. Apparently, others might disagree. Apparently I'm utterly hysterical. Everyone laughed. Everyone except Palko. And Riley. He just smiled, polite-like, which made it worse. I was mortified. Praying he would move on. But he didn't. He waits for things to settle and says: 'If you could volunteer anywhere in the world, Garnet, where would it be?'

"Everyone stared at me. And, Finch, I know this is nuts, but I couldn't think of anyplace. I don't mean I couldn't think of anyplace I wanted to volunteer. I mean, *I couldn't think of a single place in the entire world.*

"I tried to play it off. Put a finger to my lips, furrowed my brow like I was concentrating—*real* hard. I started getting hot flashy. 'Take your time,' Riley says. But Marrakech Man starts this weird giggle thing. Even Riley was embarrassed for me." She averted her eyes, as if she were back there in that moment with no way out. "There was a Beatles song on the radio. 'Octopus's Garden.' So I latch onto that. Okay, I know this. The Beatles are from . . ." She sighed. "I couldn't think of *England.*"

"You blanked out, Garnet. It happens to everyone."

"I didn't just blank out, Finch. I humiliated myself."

"You didn't. They probably didn't notice."

"Riley did. He threw me a rope. 'We have a brand new program in Costa Rica.' 'Yeah?' I say, 'Costa Rica's always been a *mega* interest of mine.' Mega? Ugh! He might just as well have said Wonderland. Or Oz. I would have volunteered for Oz in a heartbeat."

She bit down, chin out. "All I could think was: You're right, Finch."

"About what?"

"I'm totally kidding myself. If I have this baby, I'm not going anywhere. Not Mauritania. Not Tanzania. Not Ticonderoga."

"That's—what do you mean, 'if'?"

"This isn't easy—"

"What?"

"There's no good way to say it, Finch."

"Say what?"

"I'm terminating."

I cocked my head. Felt a twitchiness in the side of my face. "As in . . ."

"The pregnancy."

I slid back against the sofa, held on to the breath I had in my lungs as if it were the last gasp of oxygen on earth.

"Finch, I know you want this baby. Believe me. But I'm not ready. I don't think we are."

"This is a joke."

"If I have this baby, that's it. I'll be at Gallagher's from now until Kingdom Come. You'll be waterproofing basements 'til you're fifty. What're you doing?"

I stood at the dining room table, craning my neck so I could see up under the chandelier. "Where's the camera?"

"Finch, please."

I picked up a vase, placed it down hard. "I know there must be a camera, because this conversation can't actually be happening."

"Stop."

"Hello? TV audience?" I strolled through the galley kitchen. "You crazy sonsabitches really had me going."

"Finch!"

I emerged, sighted Garnet in my crosshairs. "I want a family."

"I do too. Just not now. Not yet."

"Now," I said. "Yet."

"I don't know how else to tell you. I'm not ready."

I unleashed an incredulous burst of air. "You said you were having this baby."

"I've been torturing myself, Finch. At first, I thought it was just nerves. I *wanted* to want this baby. There were moments I did. Just before, in the parking lot—I wasn't lying. I really thought I wanted this baby. But other feelings always come back."

"That's fear, Garnet."

"Not just. Sadness, too. And anger. At myself. At the world. Trojan, Inc. Sometimes I feel like I could rip the head off a Pound Puppy."

I walked over to her, squatted, rested my elbows on my knees, bridged my fingers, and perched my chin on them. "Garnet—this is me and you we're talking about here. Garnet and Finch. Finch and Garnet. We'll work it out."

"There's nothing to work out, Finch. I'm sorry—I really am."

"Garnet—"

"Finch."

The way she said my name—I knew she'd made up her mind. No amount of point-counterpoint could convince her otherwise.

"Where're you going?"

I slipped an arm into my jacket. "If there's nothing else to say."

"Wait," she said. "I need to ask you something."

I stood with my back to her. "It's a free country."

"This isn't easy either." She let out a breath that stretched on and on, like a timeline of the universe, and then she said: "I don't want to do this alone."

―――――

For two days, I was as lifeless as the Centerville Salt Marsh.

I logged four hundred thousand miles on my car. Listened to an entire Expos game on the radio, plus postgame commentary. I flipped through a Bible I hadn't cracked since confirmation, reread the first twenty pages of *Catcher in the Rye;* caught a double feature drive-in movie in Kyperville. I had three cups of coffee and a Danish at the Noonmark Diner.

I had told her I needed time. Twenty-four hours, though, didn't help. Monday night, I called her from a pay phone in Kyperville, between movies. The clinic was in Plattsburgh, she said—about an hour and a half away. She'd taken the first appointment they could give her: Wednesday morning at ten.

The booth flickered with preview light. "Why can't you just go alone?"

"I don't want to," she said. "This is hard enough. And they have protestors twenty-four-seven, stomping around with pictures of bloody babies and Jesus on the cross."

I shifted my jaw. "Have the baby."

"Don't start this again, Finch."

"Just think about it. For a few more days. That's all I'm asking."

"I've been thinking about it for weeks."

"So what's a few more days?"

"I won't go there, Finch. Not for a few more minutes."

The night before her appointment, when I knew Garnet would be home from her shift, I drove down the hill. Instead of turning into her parking lot, though, I kept going, out of town along the river: past Mill Stone Pier; past the cement company, its maze of ladders and crosswalks connecting giant holding tanks, lonely red lights on top, blinking out warning; through Hacksaw Flats, where sick cars went to die. At Big Bend, I crossed the river and took the sweeping turn south, plunging into a thick grove of hemlocks, birch, and pine. For a while, I couldn't see the river through the trees. Then I burst into a clearing, pulled into a turnaround, stepped out of the car. From where I stood, you could see all of Big River: the hazy swath of mine where all those garnets once rested, festooned in the folds of the earth; the college, up on the hill, its chapel spire rising in light; the brightly lit windows of houses, raining down around the campus, each one staving off someone's secret darkness.

"You're making a mistake." I was in a phone booth at the Esso station, just outside the city limits.

"I don't think so," she said.

I held the phone away from my ear, closed my eyes and dipped my chin. "You told me never to lie to you again," I said. "And I can't do this."

For a moment, I heard nothing but the crackling of lost radio waves through the wires. "Okay," she said. "Thanks for letting me know."

I woke at five A.M., guts churning like a plastic bag in an eddy. I pictured her stepping into the Trailways bus; saw her face, staring out through the glare, and, as the bus pulled away, the central station jumping from window to window, eighteen inches high. I called in sick to work. At nine thirty, I imagined her walking, head down, through a phalanx of hate. At ten, I drove to the library and returned the books I'd taken out. On the way home I stopped off at the Swenson's drive-thru. While waiting for my order, I noticed a pink corner of the homemade card peeking out from under the passenger seat. I plucked it, crumpled it into a ball. When the lady slid the window to give me my bag, I handed it over, asked her to toss it in the trash.

At home, I fell asleep on the sofa. When the phone rang, I gasped, out of my dream, bolt upright. The clock on the wall said five after five. Shadows stretched across the carpet.

"It's over," she said.

I bit down hard on my lower lip, but it didn't hurt. Most of the feeling was already gone. "You okay?"

"Been better."

"Do you want me to come over?"

"Finch," she said. "I'll be fine."

And then I heard the man's voice through the phone, and a jolt of solar wind shot through me. "Are you—is someone there?"

"Palko."

"What—what's he doing there?"

"He drove me to the clinic."

"You *told* him?"

"I didn't want to go alone."

"Yeah, but, I mean—*Palko?*"

"Listen, Finch, I'm not feeling very well. I need to go, okay? I'll call you."

She didn't, though. Not that night. And she didn't answer her phone Thursday, Friday, or Saturday. Not until Sunday afternoon. She told me I could come over, if I wanted to. When I saw her, she looked too thin, and her eyes were like the bottom of the river when a dark cloud's blocking the sun.

On the balcony, she sat in jeans and a denim jacket, a Lake Placid Olympics cap on her head, smoking a cigarette. I stood, back against the railing, facing her. She wasn't sleeping well, she said. She kept dreaming the same dream: she walks into the Food Bank storeroom, and every single shelf is bare, straight to the rafters. It's awful, Finch, she said. I reached out to touch her arm, hesitated, then let my fingers settle over her wrist, like a bracelet.

Garnet sizzle-snuffed her cigarette in rain water at the bottom of a plastic ashtray and stood, casting off my hand. She walked to the railing, rested her forearms on the metal, looked out across the river. "Listen, Finch, it's been a hard week," she said. "I think I need some time to sort things out."

"You mean—how do you mean?"

"Apart."

I licked at a skin tag on my upper lip. "Okay. Like, what, another week?"

"I don't know." She stood with her back to me, watching water run. "Maybe more."

My jaw went tight. "If you think it'll help," I said.

One week became two, and two became three. We talked every now and again on the phone, but our conversations were rudderless. When three weeks became four, I went down to Gallagher's.

The bartender said Garnet had already left. She'll be in tomorrow? I asked. No, she said. She gave notice. Yesterday was her last day.

As soon as I got home, I phoned her. She sounded up again. Not quite her normal self, but I detected a wisp of the old original Garnet, for sure. She'd been meaning to give me a call, she said. Suggested we meet for coffee at the Zone. On the way over, I felt tension evaporating from my shoulders—tension I hadn't even known was there.

She was waiting when I arrived. Our regular table was taken, so she'd found two stools at the window bar, crammed into the corner. Her hair was longer, midrange between the bob and shoulder length, and the acne had cleared up.

For a while, we made small talk. My dad was fine. Her parents, fine. Ava and her boyfriend still going strong. And then she dropped it like a stick of TNT in a mine shaft. She'd been accepted to serve in the Global Action Corps. In Costa Rica. Poverty alleviation, she said. Working with local coffee growers. They were going to pay living expenses plus a small stipend. She went on for a while about the camp she'd be living in. I was having a hard time concentrating though. I couldn't even locate Costa Rica on my mental map of the world.

"It's been so crazy, Finch," she said. "I'm leaving in two weeks."

"How long?"

"Two weeks."

"No, how long are you going for?"

"Oh, six months," she said.

"Garnet," I said. "What about us?"

She pushed her lip up to one side. "All I know is, this is right, Finch. I'm sure of it. It's what I want."

I nodded. "Wow, Garnet, this is—it's a lot to take in," I said. "It's—terrific. I'm happy for you."

A part of me probably was.

She barely touched her coffee. Mostly, she talked about how excited she was. How nervous. Riley, though, had reassured her it was a perfect fit. When she finished talking, she reached under the bar, pulled up the telescope in the case—I hadn't even noticed it down there—and handed it back to me. Thanks, she said. I enjoyed it.

Sometimes, I think about Carl Sagan's golden record, hurtling out there in space, carrying all those sounds from life on earth. I imagine an alien, happening across the record, plucking it slowly from the blackness between sucker-tipped fingers. Bringing it through a space hatch, placing it on some kind of interstellar juke-box, and then settling back in his alien easy chair to listen. He hears all sorts of interesting stuff. A mariachi band and salsa and rock 'n' roll; spoken greetings from earthlings in fifty-odd languages. He's drawn to the natural sounds: surf, wind and thunder; birds, whales, and tree frogs. And that's all great. But it strikes me that, despite NASA's best efforts, the alien doesn't really hear what matters most. Because some of the best stuff we have down here has nothing to do with those sounds and everything to do with the spaces between them.

Listen — there! — Mr. Spaceman — can you hear it? That's the sound of Big River running hard under ten inches of solid winter ice.

Listen — there! — Mr. Spaceman — that's the sound of our moon, viewed through a telescope on a cold night in spring, when the whole world smells like bean seeds punching up through wet earth.

Listen, Mr. Spaceman. And listen good. Can you hear it? Close your eyes and try harder. There! Right there! That's not what you might think. That's not nothingness. That's not anger or fear or sorrow welling up. Hold still! That's the sound of the woman you love, looking at you with a smile tugging lightly at her lips, when the very thing you want more than anything else on earth is unfolding, dreamily, before you.

Maybe he doesn't have any ears. Maybe he just listens with his skin and bones.

Big
Lake

The winter I turned thirteen, I fell in love with Molly Cage. She was my language arts teacher, who lived across Big Lake with her husband Jack, and she'd been encouraging us to think about what we wanted to do with our lives. Molly was a marathoner and health food nut who was always jogging the Indian trails around Big Lake, and with the Lake Placid Olympics one year away, I told her I wanted to be an Olympic athlete, but I needed a coach. Molly said she'd coach me, and that winter, whenever she jogged by our camp, she picked me up like a burr.

Molly wore her hair in short braids that stuck up from her head like rabbit ears, something more suited for a girl my age, and when I jogged behind her, I smelled Dial soap. We usually stopped for a break on the huge rock overlooking Catfish Cove, which was different every time we stopped, depending on the weather and time of day. Sitting there, breathing hard, we would pick out islands—some no more than a lone pine tree on the shiny crown of a boulder—name them, and give them to each other as gifts. If we were sitting close enough, that soap smell got up into my nostrils, and my mind went blank as a high December sky. I kept a running list of things to talk about in my drawer, so I wouldn't be caught short.

I liked Molly's husband, too. Jack taught forestry at Paul Smith's College, so he was around a lot during school breaks, and when Dad was at the quarry moving limestone, riprap, and gravel, I often headed over to Jack and Molly's camp. Jack would let me sort through his collection of arrowheads or hold his moose skull while Molly cooked hot cocoa from real chocolate squares.

Molly loved Big Lake even more than me. That winter, when the lake froze and ghostly ice floes bit at the curving shoreline like giant, crooked teeth, I'd sit on our pier whittling sticks and watch the smoke rising from the pipe stack above Molly and Jack's ice-fishing shed. Every now and again I hiked out to visit, but even when I didn't, I felt better just knowing she was there.

The first Saturday in March, Molly walked onto the ice at Fiddle Beach hoping to set a tip-up over her favorite walleye hole. Jack lagged behind, gathering the tackle and spud from the way-back of his station wagon, and when he looked up, the lake top was empty. For one second, maybe two, his mind didn't fathom what his eyes told him, and he yelled out her name as a question. Then he bolted onto the lake, wind lashing his face with dry power, head turning this way and that, until he spotted a wide black gash in the ice. He approached it on all fours, spreading out his weight, heart thumping. When he looked into the frigid water, he saw Molly's hat below the surface and jabbed at it. Just as he did though, the wind drove an ice floe into his arm, pinching it against the jagged lip of the lake. The doctors did all they could. Still, they had to cut off Jack's mangled arm, just below the shoulder.

Eight months later, Mom decided to have a dinner party for New Year's Eve and announced she planned to invite Jack Cage. Even worse, she asked me to hand deliver the invitation. I tried explaining to her that New Year's Eve is as useless as a bear trap in January. Everybody hates it, especially people like Jack Cage. But she said it would do Jack a world of good to be around other people instead of alone in his cabin, staring at pictures of Molly.

My sister Darcy was kneeling on a stool in the kitchen when Mom handed me the envelope, and she offered to walk with me through the woods. I told her I was taking the high route over Briar Rock instead of the longer way through the bog, so I'd better go alone. But Mom stepped in again, saying Darcy needed to get out of the house too, and Briar Rock wasn't safe in winter anyway. Darcy bunched up her shoulders like a scarecrow then dove off the stool head first, landing in a perfect handstand. She padded across the blue tiles on her hands and tucked in a somersault at the back door. Then she stood, tomato-faced, and slapped her hands together. "Race you."

"Get your mittens, Darcy," I said. "We got a long way to go."

"Don't dawdle." Mom held Frankie with one hand and mixed formula with the other. "Tell Jack we're looking forward to seeing him. Tell him Russell Shaw's coming. He's friendly with Russell."

Darcy bounded through the screen door, down three wooden steps and across the crunchy yard to the foot of the woods before stopping to catch her breath in the ice-licked air. Gypsy, our lemon-colored mutt, tore at Darcy, circled her twice, and jumped up as if she were nipping at a snowflake. Then she ran off into the forest, marking the trail. I sauntered behind, hands deep in my pockets. It was just past noon and the sky was solid white, and when we stepped into the woods, the chill came up to my ears. Darcy walked ahead, turning a long, gnarled root into a balance beam, shifting her weight this way and that with her hands held out. She reached the end, jumped off, then whirled suddenly, and bit down over her lower lip with a helter-skelter row of little teeth.

"What's the matter, Flip?"

How she knew something was eating me, I'll never know.

"Nothin'." I felt the envelope in the front of my pocket, worked it between my finger and thumb.

"Something is *too* the matter." Her pink pompom hat came right down to her eyes, making her look even younger than she was.

"So what if it is?"

"Tell." The word came out of her mouth as a simple white puff.

"The thing is, Casper"—my nickname for her since she went as the Friendly Ghost for Halloween—"I just don't know about this. About Jack."

She looked at me suspiciously, then turned back to the trail, which cut through the woods between straight-arrow spruce and pine, before curving down to meet the lake. It hadn't snowed in a few days, and you could see hard-packed dirt and pine needles. Darcy jumped into a bald patch, one-footed, teetered, then found another, and went hopscotching toward the lake.

We'd stopped going to Jack and Molly's after the accident. Darcy wanted to, but Mom wouldn't let her walk through the woods alone, and I always managed to come up with reasons for staying put. Now and then, I'd bump into Jack unexpectedly—it happened once at the Grand Union and another time at Blue Line Bait & Tackle. He always seemed excited to see me and would blabber on and on about what the smallmouth were hitting in the Saranac or a recent moose sighting in Keene Valley. As soon as I could, I'd make up a story about someplace important I had to be and then hightail it to anywhere else.

Darcy stuck a two-footed landing and spun around. "What about him?"

"It's just . . . he's turned into some kind of loner since—you know."

"Since Molly got killed."

"Yeah," I said. "Since the accident."

She watched me, lips pursed. "If he's lonesome, then maybe a party's the perfect thing."

"Let me tell you something, Darcy. Everybody hates New Year's Eve. It's the one time of year people focus on what they haven't got instead of what they have." Off to the right, in the woods, Gypsy sniffed at the twisted roots of a lightning-zapped white birch. "Imagine what it will be like for Jack."

"Mom says it'll be good for Jack."

I let out a long, hard sigh. Good for Jack, maybe. But not for me.

Here's why: Molly Cage's accident was my fault. True, a thaw had been on for over a week, but the morning before it happened the smoke-colored ice at Fiddle Beach looked solid as a concrete schoolyard. Me, Easy Ed, and Angel wanted to play hockey, so Angel went out and tested it—all two hundred crazy pounds of him. He jumped up and down and waved his arms, and we knew if the lake held through that, it'd hold for a game. There was just the matter of the sign Sheriff Pickering had posted in the parking lot: "Danger. Thin Ice. No Fishing." If there was no sign, we reckoned, how could we know not to play on the ice?

I meant to repost it afterwards—between the three of us, I was the responsible one—but Easy Ed got his fins up when Angel tripped him, and they started arguing, and, in all the excitement, I forgot.

Molly fell through the ice at noon the next day. Sheriff Pickering called it a sick joke. He put word out that whoever took the sign down would be charged with involuntary manslaughter. For a few days I was so scared I could hardly get out of bed. Then the sheriff found a burnt-out campfire, some empty beer bottles, and a few crushed packs of French cigarettes in the woods nearby, and developed a theory about a couple of Montreal backpackers who'd recently passed through town.

As soon as we heard that, the three of us met in the ruins of the old Billings house on Plevin's Point. I sat with my back against a cold stone wall, picking at red moss along the base. Angel planted himself on a crumbled corner of the hearth and watched the sky race. Easy Ed paced, kicking up leaves, lighting smoke after smoke. "It's over," he said, "if we keep our traps shut." Angel nodded, eyes filled up with clouds.

And, frankly, I was too sullen and scared to argue. I could have turned myself in and shouldered all the blame—who would have stopped me? But I was a coward, too weak willed to stand up and tell Jack: "*I'm* Pickering's 'sicko.' *I'm* the slaughterer you're looking for." Instead, I stayed quiet.

Maybe I could have left it at that, too, except that every so often, when I least expected it, the whole thing jackknifed on me.

It seemed like almost anything could trigger the memory and send me reeling. To Dad's astonishment, I couldn't bring myself to watch a single game of the Stanley Cup Finals that year. And when the family went to the winter carnival out on the lake, I made myself sick with a stomachache, just so I could stay home.

Truth was, I couldn't stand the idea of spending a night with Jack Cage in my own house, sitting with him in my living room as he watched the silver ball falling, without any way to start the old year over or stop the new one from rushing in.

"Casper, put yourself in his shoes." The path narrowed and steepened, then banked left and opened up, revealing the lake and a village of ice-fishing shanties. "Imagine what runs through his head at midnight, standing there holding a champagne glass, looking at all the couples making lovey-dovey eyes. It just might put him over."

She skidded on a patch of ice, caught herself, grabbed at a sapling. "You think?"

"I *know*."

"I don't know," she said. "Mom's making pigs in a blanket."

"Darcy, I'm serious. This isn't a time for jokes."

She stopped and whirled, hands on her hips, staring at me. "What can we do?"

"We can lose the invitation. Tell Mom we delivered it."

"You mean *lie?*"

"You don't have to lie about anything," I said. "I'll tell Mom no one answered at Jack's, so I slid it under the door. She'll never know the difference."

We watched each other for a moment, shadowed by a century-old oak, wood smoke on the still air. I thought of Angel, jumping on the ice, arms waving back and forth—in an X, then a Y, then an X—signaling that it was safe to play. "You have to trust me, Casper. Everybody hates New Year's Eve. You're just too little to know it."

She furrowed her brow. "Am *not!*"

"Then are you with me?"

She glanced across the lake. Heavy blue-gray smoke rose and spread out above the pines, where Jack lived. "Okay," she said. "I'm with you."

I pulled out the envelope. All it said was "Jack" in my mother's neat cursive. "On three we rip, got it?"

She nodded slowly, brown eyes fixed on the invitation. Then she grabbed it with her mitten, slid her tongue into the corner of her mouth. "On three."

"One." I tightened my grip. "Two . . . Three!"

We tore straight through with a sound like a striking match. I tore my half in the other direction, then put those halves together and ripped again, letting the pieces flutter to the snow. Darcy held her half with two hands, staring at it. Then she pulled both hands away at once, as if it had caught fire.

We walked a little further into the woods, to kill time. Darcy got quiet, shuffling her feet through the snow, watching the ground.

"We should turn around," I said. "It's getting dark."

"Flip?" Darcy kicked at a triangle of thin snow that had crusted over a rock like a pope hat. "Remember that time Molly showed us how to catch a chipmunk in a box?"

I nodded.

She looked at me, blinked, and ran the back of her mitten across her leaky nose. "She used to make the best hot chocolate in the world."

My mouth juiced up. "We better get back, Casper." I glanced at the sky over their camp. Then I closed my eyes and remembered the chipmunk in the Charmin box, ricocheting against the cardboard walls in an all-out brainless panic, until Jack lifted the chicken wire and set it free.

"Where's Darcy?"

It's funny how a simple question can jump-start your heart.

Mom had just set a bowl of ruffled chips on the coffee table when she remembered Darcy. I'd been too busy spreading rock salt and carrying firewood to realize she was gone. Dad had taken Frankie to McCafferty's to pick up a few more bottles of bubbly. The guests were due to start arriving at any time.

"Did she go with Dad?"

"She was here arranging chairs." Mom called up the landing. "Darcy?" She walked out onto the back porch. "Darcy?"

"I'll go look for her, Mom. I'm sure she's around here some-where."

"I told her not to go anywhere."

"Don't worry. She's probably just out playing."

I pulled on my boots, jacket, and gloves, and made straight for the woods, looking back once. Mom stood on the porch with no coat, cradling herself. Behind her, every window glowed with or-ange light, and the chimney sent a charcoal swirl into a shale-colored sky.

I knew where Darcy'd gone. She'd spent the whole week mop-ing and, at one point, had tried to convince me that ripping up the invitation was "a bad thing" — even worse than stealing gobstop-pers from Cumberland Farms, which I'd done once on a dare. It wasn't too late, Darcy said. We could still invite him. When I told her we'd done everyone an enormous favor by ripping up the en-velope, she threatened to tell Jack, herself. I didn't think the little nun would actually go through with it, but the second Mom put out the APB, I knew I'd underestimated her.

The only question was: could I catch Darcy before she got to Jack's? She would have gone the long way, through the bog. If I took the short cut over Briar Rock, I could head her off.

I walked, fast as I could between the trees, sun slipping like an egg yolk in the sky. When my digits started freezing, I balled my fists inside my gloves, letting the glove fingers go floppy. Before long, I had to reinsert my fingers so I could move aside prickle bushes and branches, but the gloves had nearly frozen solid, and the cold shot through my elbows like a reverse funny-bone zap. I thought about the "Stages of Frostbite" poster on the wall of the nurse's office at school, showing how skin goes from beige to pink to red to black and blistery, and then I started singing an old rhyme about a lion hunt, just to knock the pictures out of my head.

I pressed up the hill, moving faster as the air grew thinner and the trees grew smaller, until I came to the steepest part of the rock. I found my path and worked my way up into a familiar groove, using tree roots and jutting cuts of boulder to pull myself along. When I reached the top, I stood, stretched, wiped dirt and snow from my jeans.

The lake top was a carpet of cloud. Stunning whiteness spread before me, drowning everything in light. Standing on the ledge, wind swirling, I let my eyes blur and spread my arms like wings. And for a moment, I was flying above the lake, the same lake that had swallowed Molly Cage in a silent, icy gulp.

The scream came from behind me. It rose to a horrifying pitch, and, just as it trailed off, folded over on itself, softer, ghostlike. It died, abruptly, then rose up again, echoing off the rock face. I recognized Darcy and bolted from the ledge, propelled by fear and the wind. I peered into the slanting woods, saw nothing, and started down, knees absorbing the slope, hands out against the tilt, ahead of an avalanche of pebbles and ice. At the bottom, rounding a large boulder, I almost tripped over her, on her side in the snow, whimpering softly, holding her leg.

"Darcy! Jesus Christ! Are you okay?"

"Flip!" She looked up at me. "You're here!"

"What happened?"

"I was . . . I wanted Jack—" She tried to prop herself on her palms, winced, and fell against the snow with a low moan.

"Jesus, Darcy, don't move for Christ's sake!"

"Help me, Flip. It hurts."

"What hurts?"

"Everything."

"What hurts most?"

"My foot," she reached down, held behind her knee, where her jeans had ripped. "My *ankle*."

I pushed up her jeans. The skin disappearing into her boot was burned and scraped, flecked and seared with small white stones. There was no bone showing—that was good—but Darcy's face was as white as the Olympic mountain, and it scared the crap out of me. If she went into shock, we were goners.

"Okay, just listen," I said. "You're gonna be fine. Hear me?"

"I want Mommy."

I held her at the shoulders. "I said: 'Do you hear me?'"

"I'm *cold*, Flip."

I spotted her hat, off in the woods, retrieved it, and pulled it down carefully over her hair and red-rimmed ears. Brushed a small clump of dirt from her cheek.

"Man, Casper. You're something else, you know that? You almost made it over the steepest rock in Franklin County."

Darcy tried a smile, coughed, shut her eyes.

I took off my glove. Touched the back of my hand to her forehead.

Clammy. Too cold.

"Listen, Casper. I'm gonna pick you up like this"—I held my hands out, palms up, as if delivering a serving tray—"I need you to stay as still as you can? Got it?"

She nodded.

I slid one hand under her knees. She leaned forward so I could slide the other under her neck.

"*Ouch*," she whispered.

"I'll have you home in no time flat."

Then gently, as if I were picking up my baby brother, I rose from my knee, cupping Darcy in my arms. Before I was even upright, though, she shrieked and screamed and kicked her bad leg out, and I lowered her straight back to the ground.

"What's *wrong*?"

"It hurts! Oh, Flip. Am I gonna die?"

"Casper, you're not gonna die. Your ankle's twisted. Maybe broke. But you're not gonna die."

She put her cheek down against the snow and groaned.

I knew what I'd have to do. There are times when a thought can break your heart. And that's what happened to me, standing there, trying to figure out how I was going to tell her. I glanced up through a gap in the pines. The sky held another thirty minutes of daylight, at most. I felt in my pockets for matches, hoping I could light a small fire to help keep her warm, but came up empty. I had to move.

"Listen, Casper." I crouched, touched her forehead. "The quickest way . . ."

"No, Flip . . ." She raised herself up on her elbows. "You can't leave me."

"I have to, Darcy."

"I'll die," she said. "I promise you, I'll die."

"I have no choice."

"They'll come for us. They'll send a search party."

"We'll freeze to death first."

She launched herself at me, wrapping both hands around my

ankle. Gripped me tighter than I ever thought she could. "I won't let you go."

I peeled her mittens apart and stood. "I don't have time for this, Darcy."

"Flip!" she screamed. "I hate you!"

I took my jacket off and laid it over her, avoiding her eyes. Then I turned, heading for the cliff side.

"Don't leave me," she said, almost a whisper.

I'd only taken a few steps when I heard the sound, low and far off, a soft purring rumble like a distant chain saw slicing timber. I stopped, shook my head hard, and the sound went away. It came back, though, steady and unmistakable.

I whirled. "Darcy, listen. Hear that?"

"What?"

"*Shhhhhhhh*. Listen."

"Flip!"

"Yeah." I shook my head. "Someone's on the lake."

"Hurry!" Her voice was all hope. "Please!"

I bolted across the trail and ran down a hill to the icy lake edge. Stepped onto the whiteness, past the slanting shadows of tilted trees, and waved my arms frantically at a red snowmobile hurtling across the ice from a cove on the far bank. "Here!" I shouted. "Over here! *Help*!"

And as the yards between us melted away and the roar of the engine throttled the air, I saw the slick orange visor curving across the white helmet and the sleeve of a winter jacket flapping wildly in the wind, empty.

It took us until after dark working with three arms and an Eveready flashlight to get Darcy back to the house. When Jack pulled the snowmobile alongside our dock, Darcy trailing behind in his wood sled, the party guests were already waiting at the top of the hill in a thick huddle. Jack cut the engine, and they ran at us, as if the house were draining into the lake. In the flood of the back porch halogen, I saw Doc Singh striding ahead of the rest, arms pumping. Mom had invited him to the party, too.

We took Darcy inside and laid her on the couch in front of the muted TV, showing pictures of Times Square as it filled up. Doc Singh worked off her boot, gentle as ginger ale. All you could see was a sock with smiling bunny faces. He pressed on her ankle, rotating her foot this way and that, and she scrunched her eyes and bared her teeth, but I could tell—she was sponging up the sympathy.

"Well, Darcy." He spoke with an Indian accent. "I think we've got a pretty bad sprain on our hands here. Plus a minor abrasion. Let's get some ice on it. You'll be fine."

With that, the room filled back up with air. I forced off my boots and wiggled my toes to facilitate a thaw. Everyone sat, and a measure of relief washed over me, until someone asked what the hell had happened.

"Darcy fell," I said. "Briar Rock." Then I tossed out a gem. "She was out looking for Gypsy." Her eyes fluttered and closed. "We flagged Jack down on the lake."

Mom turned to Jack. "We figured you'd come over land, but I guess we ought to thank you for choosing the snowmobile. These kids would have frozen solid."

Jack held Mom's gaze. The only sound came from the hearth, where the wood sap sizzled and sparked. I figured my ride was over. I'd run out of ways to stretch the truth, and even the stomach to keep trying. I looked down at my socks. There was a purple stain over the big toe from the time I tore my nail skateboarding Ampersand Hill.

"I was planning to drive," Jack said, "but at the last minute I decided on the lake. Call it 'providence.'" He smiled, and when I looked up—I swear on Angel's Indian stone—he was staring right at me. *Providence?* What the hell was he pulling?

I looked at Jack, really took him in. The last time I'd truly *seen* him was on TV, a few weeks after the accident. A girl reporter asked how it felt to lose his wife, and my whole family sat around, Mom and Dad hushing each other so they could hear the gory details, but all I could think was: *How the hell do you think it feels, Lois freaking Lane?* Man, he'd aged like cheese in the sun since then. He had thin gray hair, shooting off his freckled scalp at crazy angles. His face was too thin, pale skin sagging from his jowls as if it had given up. His eyes, gray as a steelhead's back, had lost their starry light, and he stooped noticeably. About the only thing the same was his outfit—orange lumberjack flannel, tan corduroy pants, and tan work boots.

Mom blinked at him. "Isn't that true," she said. "Amen to that."

"I'll tell you what." Mayor O'Boyle sat on Dad's easy chair, feet up on the ottoman, sipping a cocktail. "That was a heroic effort out there, Jack Cage. Folks could learn a thing or two from you."

That seemed to be everyone's cue—it was okay to start the party. Guests helped themselves to chicken potpie and Mom's famous diner mac 'n' cheese, then sat on couches and folding chairs, staking out card table space for plastic plates and beer bottles, and began regaling each other with stories about near misses in the forest. The time O'Boyle got caught in a hailstorm on Mount Marcy with a barbershop quartet from Racine. The time Russell Shaw got lost surveying the perimeter of Old Man Peachtree's estate, surviving for two days on wintergreen, white pine bark, and creek water. Stories we'd all heard umpteen times. Jack told the one about Maurice Jesperson, who got stranded on a breakaway ice floe and had to be rescued by the fire department. Everyone laughed. Jack seemed pretty pleased with himself. He was acting as if Molly had just stepped outside for a breath of mountain air and would be walking in through the side door any minute, her skin fresh and cold.

By the time Mom brought out the joe and the sharp smell of cooked coffee beans swirled in from the kitchen, my chest felt tight as a well-thrown spiral. Dick Clark came on TV. His mouth moved and smiled, smiled and moved, wordless. Mom put a tray on the coffee table with a carafe, sugar bowl, creamer, and a dozen or so mugs, then sat on the couch, stroking Darcy's forehead. The mayor walked over to Jack, standing near a table of card players. Doc Singh and Herman Miller, the general store–keeper, were damn near spellbound by a story Jack'd been telling about chestnut blight. Russell Shaw shook his head from side to side and whistled. His girlfriend Mary all but had tears in her eyes.

I sat for a while, arms crossed, eyeing Jack the way a wise old bass would eye a hula popper. Something in my gut told me he knew about the sign. I kept thinking about the moment, a few hours before, when I'd realized it was *Jack* speeding toward me on Big Lake. The white sun glinted off his visor and his machine screamed like a prehistoric bird, trailing thick smoke as it smashed through moguls, teetering from ski to ski. Jack smiled through clenched, frozen teeth. For a second, I'd forgotten all about Darcy and I turned suddenly, to run. I caught myself after a half step, but Jack had seen me flinch. Surely that was enough for him to deduce the whole horrible truth.

In the living room, Gypsy got up from in front of the fire, walked into the hall, and sat by the front door. She growled softly, steaming a glass pane with her nostrils, staring into the blackness as if there were something shadowy coming up the walk. I muttered something about her needing to go—no one cared—and then pulled on my boots, pushed open the door, and followed her out.

"I know how you feel, girl," I said.

I walked behind her in the still night, across the snow-crusted yard, and stood in a small pool of yellow porch light. Muffled laughter rose from inside, Jack's deep bellow climbing above the din.

At the edge of the forest, I spotted a semi-deflated soccer ball, peeking out from under a hood of snow, abandoned where it'd stopped rolling after the final kick of a dismal summer. I charged, my boots crashing through the icy crust, and kicked the ball in full stride with a solid *whump*, launching it into the forest in a blizzard of cracking twigs and exploding snow.

Gypsy lifted her nose and looked at me, panting. Then she ambled off toward the woods herself.

"Come on, girl," I said. "Party's over."

Back in the living room, the crowd around Jack had grown. Anita Devorah, the local real estate agent, had muscled her way into the circle and stood, black hair cascading to her waist, listening to Jack with a gleam in her eye. Jack said something, and surprise plastered her face, wide as a truck flap. Then Jack said something else, and she nodded like a well-tended jig, hair rising and falling. Eventually, Russell and Mary and Doc Singh drifted off. After laying out his entire platform, the mayor walked away, too. That's when Anita Devorah put her arm around Jack's waist and leaned in real close—close enough that her words could have tickled his neck. She squeezed his side and hit him with a frisky look, and a frozen feeling ran straight through me.

I scanned the room. Everyone was oblivious.

After a few seconds, Anita Devorah released Jack's waist and pulled away, nodding. Jack let loose a laugh that rattled the floorboards. Something inside me gave.

"What the hell is so funny?" A dozen heads turned, all eyes on me. I locked onto Jack's. "Would you mind telling me what the hell you have to be so happy about?"

Jack looked at me as if I'd just peppered his dog with buckshot.

"Molly's dead, for Christ's sake," I said. "She's dead."

Then I chose the only option I had left. I ran. Through the living room, into the front hall, and out of the house. I ran, beneath a full moon, down the salted driveway to the dirt road, and out to the highway. I slipped, fell, picked myself up, and ran some more, kicking up sand and road salt, cold air smacking my lips. Eventually, I found the Indian trail and cut into the forest. When I got to the rock at Catfish Cove, I fell down on all fours and cried.

I don't know how long I stayed that way. A lot came out of me, heaving up. I cried until my ribs hurt, letting the tears drop straight to the rock and freeze.

When I heard the snowmobile, I took a deep breath, looked up. It came at me on a line from the lake, engine rising, headlight brimming gold. The drone increased, louder and louder, until it drowned out my own breathing. The orb of light disappeared beneath curving rock. The engine cut, I caught a whiff of diesel, and then, a moment later, a light beam slashed up from the forest, slicing through trees. Before long, it honed in on me, sprawled across the rock face, shivering, and I raised my arm against the blindness.

"Thought I'd find you here." Jack took off his jacket, draped it over my shoulders. It was warm and smelled of gasoline and wood smoke. Of him.

I sat up, palms pressed into the cold stone. Ran Jack's sleeve across my nose. He sat next to me, stretched his legs out across the rock, switched off his light. The lake popped with moonlight.

"What's going on, Flip?"

"What's going on is Molly's dead. She's dead and nobody cares."

"I care."

"No, you don't. You *don't* care. How can you laugh like that?"

Jack shifted against the boulder and let out a slow breath. "Molly's been dead nearly a year, Flip," he said. "We have to get on with it."

"Not me."

"All of us."

"Why?"

"What choice do we have?"

I let out a short, clipped breath, put my head to my arms, looked down at the rock. I might've been thinking of a name for an island. The one with the two pines touching, or the other, by the tributary, that was always disappearing in the mist.

"I killed Molly, Jack."

"What?"

"*I* killed her. Not a drunk guy from Montreal. Not some stupid tourist. *Me!*"

Jack's body went rigid next to mine. "Molly drowned, Flip. Under the ice."

"I took down the *sign*! We wanted to play hockey, so I took it down. *Me!*" I tilted my head back and shouted at the sweeping black sky: "*Me! I did it!*"

Jack shook his head slowly and exhaled a breath that smelled of cheese doodles and cheap champagne. He raised his arm, and I flinched — in my mind, I'd already seen him cock a fist, rear back, and slam his knuckles against my skull — but he only scratched at a dandruffy patch of scalp. "So it was you. All this time."

I shook my head weakly. "Yeah."

"I suppose that's it then."

"That's it."

"And what's the penalty for sign removal these days?" He raised a bushy gray eyebrow. "Twenty-five to life? Or're they just sending perps straight to the chair?"

My heart rose up in my chest. "Jack, I wasn't thinking straight. I never thought . . ."

"Come on, Flip. I'm joking. What are you telling me? *You* killed Molly? That's hogwash and you know it."

"But Sheriff Pickering said . . ."

"Sheriff Pickering's an old man with too much time to kill. That sign had nothing to do with it. Everyone knew about the thaw. They'd been broadcasting warnings on North Country Radio all week. Molly and I talked about it. She said the forecasters were being overly cautious. We had at least another day to fish. Maybe two."

"But if you'd seen the sign . . ."

"It wouldn't have mattered, Flip. Molly'd made up her mind. Nothing would have stopped her."

"It was a big sign," I said. "In the parking lot. Danger. Thin Ice."

"We knew, Flip."

I held my eyes wide open against the searing cold air, resisting the urge to blink, until light and dark shapes merged across the lake. "If you knew," I said, "why'd you let her go?"

Jack gripped my shoulder with his fingers spread, turning me toward him. He looked at me, and something flashed in his eyes I didn't recognize. Something distant and fleeting, like lightning. Then he laughed the way you laugh when nothing in the whole wide world is funny.

"What was I supposed to do, Flip? Lock her up?"

"Yes!"

"And throw away the key?"

"*Yes!*"

"That would've worked?"

I shrugged, hopeless, miserable. Bit my lip.

He moved his arm across my shoulder and pulled me into him, letting me feel his strength. For a while, he didn't say anything. "I think about her all the time, Flip," he said, finally, his voice soft but firm. "I was remembering something just today I hadn't thought about in a while. I'm not sure what made me think of it. That's the way it goes with Molly. She comes at me sometimes when I'm chopping wood."

His looked straight up at the Milky Way, squinting, as if he expected to locate her up there in the haze.

"We're fishing Panther Pond one morning. Steam's rising off the water, and we're cutting it like a plane through clouds. Can't see more than a few feet in any direction. The only sound is the oars breaking the pond top, smooth as glass. Molly's got a Lake Clear Warbler fifty feet below the boat, trailing a crawler. And I can see by her eyes she's down there with the bait, like she always was.

"It was one of those frustrating days. We'd been out for hours and tried every lure known to man, without a single hit. I was hot and tired. My arms ached. I wanted to knock off and go home, but Molly—Molly had a feeling. 'Just one more cast,' she said. And one more turned into one more, and so on. You know how it was with her."

I nodded. "I *know*."

"I was just about to head in despite her when she held her hand out, eyes on her rod tip. Nothing seemed unusual to me. But she held a finger to her line. Watched it as if it were alive. A few seconds went by and nothing. I asked her if she had a hit, and she put her finger to her lip to shut me up. It wasn't the first time. I figured—to hell with her. I stopped rowing, massaged my shoulder, let the breeze take the boat sideways a measure. But before I could dip the oars and start in, she hauled back on the line and set the hook, rod bent like a rainbow." He shook his head. "Ten minutes later, I'm slipping the net over a thirty-inch laker."

"Thirty inches!"

"Maybe more."

"On a *Warbler*?"

He nodded. "It was one beautiful fish. Brown across the back, almost gold, with white speckles."

I shook my head, imagining. Trout that size are the stuff of legend in Big Lake.

"And you know what she does?" Jack looked at me. "She holds the fish with two hands, and before I can so much as peep, she lowers it into the water. Gives it right back to the lake."

"She let it go?"

"Let it go."

"She didn't even weigh it?"

"Nope."

"No pictures."

"Not a one." He shook his head. "She just looked at me and said we should head in. As if it were her idea."

"She could have had that fish *stuffed*."

"It was a damn fool thing."

A whippoorwill unleashed a brief, haunting song into the forest, and I leaned against him.

"I miss her, Jack. I miss her so much it hurts."

"I do, too, Flip," he said. "I miss her, too."

"I wish we could have her back."

Jack didn't speak. So I waited. Waited until I got my breath. Waited as the wind drew a tracer of cloud across the face of the moon. When I finally looked up, Jack was staring across the lake at something I couldn't see.

We stayed that way awhile, listening to the frozen quiet. Every so often a twig cracked in the forest, an unseen animal giving us the once-over with a sniffle. Jack took in deep, even breaths that made me think he was far away. And then I heard the ticking of his watch and turned his wrist to the moonlight. It was just a few seconds before midnight.

I didn't know then that Jack had already put his camp up for sale or that Anita Devorah had an offer from a rich New Jersey banker looking for a summer home, willing to pay cash. I had no idea that when the spring term ended, Jack would pack up a U-Haul with all his belongings and head out to his mother's in California, leaving Darcy and me behind for a place with fewer ghosts. How could I have known those things? And how could I have known that years later, Molly would still haunt me?

What I did know, sitting there under the still trees of Catfish Cove, is that for once, I was exactly where I wanted to be. I closed my eyes, and from far off in the distance came the faint roar of the crowd, rolling into the dark valley like a thunderclap, a million mouths open in a giant, hopeful scream. And then, hovering above a glittering, drunken city, bathed in the bright lights of Times Square, the silver ball finally began to fall, sliding closer to tomorrow with each passing second.

The
Carousel

I've been a carousel man for thirty-three years.
I work the "B & D Carousell" on Surf Avenue—one of the originals manufactured by William F. Mangels—which my father
operated before me. When my father started up in the business,
there were twenty-odd full-sized wooden carousels on Coney
Island, but mine's the only one left. There are a lot of reasons for
this, and I'm happy to give you the main one. Kids are different
these days. They'd rather sit in a cave somewhere and twiddle a
joystick than take a ride on a calliope.

"Whether or not a carousel makes you rich, Rubin, it can sometimes make you happy." That's what my father told me the day he
handed me the keys to the crankshaft on my twenty-fifth birth-

day. And that's the way it was for me. I had started out as a ring boy when I was thirteen, and even back then, the B & D was a one of a kind. It had a sixty-six-key Gebruder organ, thirty-six jumping horses, fourteen standers, and two chariots—figures whittled by the legendary artists from the Brooklyn school of carousel carving—and stainless steel rings that riders could grab for.

The sideshow guys used to say that I had the sand in my shoes, and I suppose that's true in a sense. All I ever needed was Coney Island. I worked hard in the summer months and stayed open weekends from November to April, making a few bucks here and there, enough to hang on to an apartment in Flatbush. My sister—my only family to speak of—died a spinster the year I celebrated my thirtieth anniversary as a carousel man, and after that, all I had was the B & D, but I never missed any other kind of life.

On one particular Saturday, not long after my sister had passed, I got to work early, feeling restless. Truth was, after all those years, I was thinking about shutting the carousel down for good. I'd recently removed the brass ring because I couldn't afford to give out free rides anymore, and I still couldn't make it pay, even on $2.50 a ride. A buddy of mine knew of a job at the Port Authority, taking tickets on the ferry. It wasn't much, he said, but it was steady.

The weather that day was Coney Island first week of November, back when the month still had something to do with it. I started the morning like any other, by wiping the chalkboard clean, a ritual I'd come to respect over the years. Then I took a fresh piece of white chalk and wrote "B & D Carousell"—the spelling preferred by Mr. Mangels—plus "156 Days 'Til Easter" and "Rides $2.50."

By late afternoon, Surf Avenue was empty. Not a single kid had shown up all day, and I had run out of excuses regarding the grand chariot, a figure contributed by master craftsman George Carmel. Several of the carriage's curved wooden planks had separated, and to fix them, I knew I'd have to get inside so I could see what else had rotted away. I had been meaning to do the work for some time.

A gusty breeze kicked up as I stepped onto the calliope, and sand kernels *ticked* against the horses. I made my way through the herd until I reached Belinda, grand chariot in tow, her head held a notch higher than the other ponies, and I smiled at her, just like a school kid would. But I didn't let myself dally. I stepped into the carriage with some difficulty, owing to a lower back problem that was beyond the realm of modern medicine. Adjusting my weight on the bench, I stretched my legs forward and leaned back under the roof. All sounds from the outside world cut off—so abruptly it startled me.

The chariot right off the top seemed small to me, much smaller than I remembered. My knees bent awkwardly into the planking, and my elbows chafed the sides. How long had it been since I'd been inside? Twenty years? More? Could this have been the same chariot where I once took my girls on date night? I raised my worn hand and touched the wooden mermaid carved into the bridge. I remembered staring at this fish girl when I was sixteen, back when she still had diamonds for eyes, and asking myself, *Should I kiss Melanie Mendelsohn?* I know it sounds crazy, but it was as if the mermaid spoke to me and told me to do it, a thing that until that moment I was sure I could not do. Now the mermaid's face was barely a face, smoothed down over the years by the beating wind; the green wooden scales had chipped and flaked away, and the tail was cracked lengthwise. I rubbed my thumb over the soft wood, lingering in the empty eye sockets.

My back started aching, so I flattened myself lower into the chariot and craned my neck, peering into the hood of the thing, looking for white shavings of daylight where the planks had popped. I saw nothing and tried to shift; my neck muscles clutched at my shoulders in a spasm. When I looked up, I saw the roof of the carriage, curling over me like a wave, blocking out the daylight.

That's when I was overcome with it: spinning. The carousel had started to turn. I quickly pulled myself from inside the pod and leapt out, but as soon as my feet hit the platform I realized I was wrong. The B & D was completely still. I reached out for a jumper to steady myself and closed my eyes. When I opened them, I saw a boy standing on the sand at the edge of the calliope. I was surprised to see him there alone. Over the years, crime around those parts had gotten pretty bad.

"Hello, Mr. Polonsky," he said. "Are you open?"

He couldn't have been more than nine or ten. He wore a collared brown jacket with wooden buttons, and his hair was slicked back with something like brilliantine, which seemed strange for such a little guy. But the thing that really got me was his voice. It was as if he said every word twice, a fraction of a second apart, so that his sentences were out of register. It sounded as though he were talking underwater.

"Sure am, kid," I said, jumping off.

He held out a dime, and I couldn't help myself. I laughed. The carousel hadn't cost a dime in forty years. I looked out across the road toward the ocean. An old woman passed by on a green bicycle and smiled. "That's okay. It's on the house today."

The boy blinked, shoved the dime into his pocket, and stepped up onto the wooden planks. He searched out his pony carefully, touching haunches, petting wooden snouts. Finally he settled on Bella, a blue-eyed jumper, which was not a bad choice at all. I cranked her up and let her go, and she started with a shudder, first time moving in a week. Organ music drifted down West 12th Street on a soft breeze from the ocean. I sat back in my folding chair and watched her spin.

The kid held on to the golden pole and leaned forward like a modern-day Lone Ranger. What struck me as he went around, rising and falling, was his laughter. It was a laughter as pure as any I'd ever heard, edging toward fear, but with a musical quality. It was as if several people were laughing, instead of only one, and it reminded me of something, although at that time, I couldn't say just what.

When the ride ended, he slid off his pony, wove through the horses, and leapt off the platform with two feet.

"Thank you, Mr. Polonsky," he said. "That was terrific."

He turned to go.

"Hey, kid, wait a minute," I said. "Do I know you?"

"Sure, Mr. Polonsky," he said. "I come here a lot."

I shook my head. In the summer, it was pretty crowded. And he definitely looked familiar, although I made it a point of pride to remember the names of the regulars. "Oh, yeah, sure," I said. "Well, it's good to see you again."

The kid smiled.

"Where's your mom, kid? You live around here? You need me to call you a cab?"

He wrinkled his eyebrows. "Why, she's just there," he pointed toward the vacant lots where the old sideshows used to be, dark beyond the orange glow of the carousel. "She's with my sister. It's her birthday."

I nodded. "Be careful," I said.

"Thanks again, Mr. Polonsky," he said. And then he turned and ran, his soft shoes tamping down the sand.

I shook my head and let out a short breath. "Crazy kids," I said.

It was then that I first noticed the smell, air-popped caramel corn, and for some reason it didn't occur to me to wonder about it, even though the vendors had stopped coming years before. The boy ran toward the gate, and as he did, he passed the chalkboard. That's when it caught my eye — written there in white chalk, in my father's simple hand: "Rides 10 Cents."

When I looked up, the boy had disappeared into the dark, wind-swept street. I stood and ran toward the gate. I thought about my father just then. *It can sometimes make you happy.* For an instant, I heard the sound of a carnival on the breeze — the distant cry of a lonely barker and the laughter of young love. Then, as quickly as it had come to me, it was gone.